# A Hopeless MEDIA 3

# THE NEMESIS

BRIAN PHILLIPS

This is a work of fiction. Names, characters, places, and incidents either are the product of the author's imagination or are used fictitiously. Any resemblance to actual persons, living or dead, events, or locales is entirely coincidental.



ISBN: 979-8-9888986-2-7



First edition: Published Summer 2024

Book cover designed by Peter L (Okomota) of Fiverr

Book layout by Pooja Mehra (Aalishaa) of Fiverr

# From the Author:

A Hopeless Media 3 – The Nemesis is the third installment in The Hopeless Media trilogy, and picks up where the prior installment left off. Book 1 laid the foundation for world building and character development. Book 2, *The Hit*, continued the journey for Shane and the others as they endured various intense and traumatic events on their journey. I am including the content warning from the other books in the series below:

*Content Warning: This book series depicts numerous intense and traumatic scenarios. All victims and survivors of traumatic life experiences should know that they are not alone. This series is dedicated to those who have felt their voices silenced by the world around them. While it will contain graphic scenarios heavy enough to cause triggers, there are also those who will be reading this who have never experienced certain scenarios themselves. The hope is that by walking in the shoes of these characters that they will be able to understand what is happening behind the facade of our society, and to awaken our empathy toward humanity. For those who have experienced these scenarios, they know all too well that life does not sugar coat it; that there is an evil in this world that seeks to thrust humanity into oblivion. The only thing that can transcend this evil... is love.*

# CHAPTER 1

# The Recruit

*August 20, 2045*

A few days ago, my mom and I finally got to meet with Hailey's parents in more than just passing. We invited them over for dinner, and Bernice provided my mom with the ingredients needed to make a hearty beef stew. Contrary to the common stereotype that introverts can't hold a conversation, both of them were actually quite alright in doing so. They are in their mid-50s and waited until their late 30s to have Hailey. Her dad, Tim, upholds a majority of the administrative aspects of their landscaping business, while her mom, Amber, works on the planning and design of their work. Hailey often assists them both with the actual work and gets paid under the table for doing it.

The Burnett elders have been long aware of our activity in AURORA, as Hailey told them in an effort to be transparent. They seemed like the type who would have restricted her much like Gary's parents did with him, but by the time we had joined AURORA, Hailey had already turned 18 and they felt that they had no choice but to allow her to make her own decisions as an adult. Of course, when the topic of the isolation ward incident came up, they confessed that right then and there they were trying to pull the plug on Hailey's participation, which explained a lot about her distance at the time. However, eventually Hailey said that she wanted to "make things right" by fighting the very system that allowed such an atrocity to occur in the first place, so that others would not endure the same fate that she did. My mom had chimed in as well with her experience with Bergeron in 2026, the same year that Hailey was born.

It came to my attention as well that Tim and Amber both know Norm Bigelow's son, Troy, who was one of their customers recently, and he is also a current employee at the police station. Troy is not so fond of Officer Bergeron either, and he told them that he would "exploit any vulnerability" if the opportunity came up. It was comforting to know that we had an ally on the inside. This also explained who gave Mr. McFarlane "permission" to take a plane to New York. The Burnetts said that they supported our cause, but wanted to stay out of the spotlight because of their business. Her dad mentioned that on the bright side, they could keep communication with Troy, and Hailey can be the messenger, without drawing attention to either of them. This was a win-win scenario for all of us involved.

Today was just another boring Sunday. My mom and I sat near the back of the church. I wasn't sure about her, but I was less than enthusiastic to be here and, quite honestly, my mind was anywhere but here. My only reason for going was to keep my mom company and nothing more. I had too much on my mind lately, particularly with the day to day dynamic between Shannon and the rest of the group. So far Mr. McFarlane and Pablo have been able to keep her in check, and she and Hailey have yet to get into an all-out cat fight. But I would definitely not rule out the possibility of them getting into it. Shannon and my mom have actually had a few interesting conversations though, whether some passing comments about my father or the fact that they have had a somewhat similar history. I was present for one of the conversations which pertained to my grandparents that I never met. While Shannon's parents were pretty much exhibitionists, my mom's parents were religious bigots. Judgmental, self-righteous, prude, and narcissistic. The very idea of "intimacy" itself, however one may interpret the word, might as well have been a sin. It was the perfect recipe for hypocrisy. The more they pushed my mom, the more she pulled away. She ran away and pretty much was just like Shannon in her younger years, at least outwardly. My mom would engage in sexual relations rather quickly with *anyone* who would show her any kind of attention or affection because sex was her way of trying to fill the void left by her parents neglect. She had no intention to hurt anyone, only that she was looking for love and acceptance in all the wrong places due to her low self-esteem. Then came my dad.

My father, being the understanding man that he was, had profound emotional maturity for his age because my grandfather (may he also rest in peace) was a man of immense wisdom and intelligence. My grandpa warned my dad not to try to "fix a damaged person", but my dad, a fixer by nature, couldn't help himself and would end up falling in love with the woman. I guess he was one of the lucky ones. Over time and with patience, my mom began to trust him more, and the rest was history. My mom told me that it doesn't always end up that way, and that much of the time, it doesn't. For the longest time she thought my dad was simply too good to be true. But then my brother was killed, and my dad was the one to hold my mom together through that. When my dad was killed, that responsibility fell to me, whether I was ready for it or not. I'd like to hope that I am my father's son, but my repository of wisdom is lacking in comparison to what his was. Under pressure I still make dumb decisions. I don't have all the answers. I think I am better than I was, but I still have a lot of work to do. It doesn't help that my past mistakes have been eating away at my conscience.

My mom for the longest time resented church and, because of her parents, she wanted absolutely nothing to do with God or Jesus or any of the like. She had only turned back to God because of my dad. Today, we both feel the same way with church, being in an absolute cold spell, but knowing that my dad is waiting for us on the other side, when our lives are over here, we would hate to miss him. It's like they say, you have to "be good" in order to go to Heaven… whatever the heck that's supposed to mean. For the both of us, it seems that "church" is still only a means to an end. My understanding was that it was supposed to be more about community than anything else.

It just so happened that the topic of Pastor Kevin Lohan's sermon was "Intentions". Years of lukewarm feelings toward routine Sunday mornings was a long, dark tunnel where no light dared to shine. I had yet to see anything happen that would make me be anything more than cynical about life. It kept my mom's weary thread of hope intact, however, and I didn't want her to face her demons alone. It killed me to see her become a basket case whenever things became dire, which they often did. I had to offer my support wherever I could.

"We all suspect people we know to be quote un-quote fake." The pastor preached in his usual cheesy manner. "Nice to everyone in their faces but deep inside, they carry that envy, that jealousy, or even resentment for those that they claim to care about. But folks, good works without faith is dead. You can't just 'work' your way to Jesus. God will not accept you just going through the motions. You have to do it like you *mean* it. Intention. *Intention* is the root of all activity. *Intention* is where the heart stands. *Intention* tells all of existence… if your heart is really in this."

He made a raised fist motion as he said "mean it". This speech felt like it was directed at me. Lately I *have* been just "going through the motions". Perhaps that's why a lot of crazy shit has been happening to me recently. Everything in my life right now was lacking passion, and almost always was a means to some kind of end. But in the end, I wondered if I was merely squandering my time being angry about things that I have no control over. Sure, I'm a doer, like my father before me. I like to get things done, but the real question is "why am I doing it?"

"It has been said in many ways." the pastor continued, pacing slowly a few steps back and forth behind the podium in his charcoal gray suit. "God loves a cheerful giver. John 20:29 says blessed are those who haven't seen me, but believe. Let's take the story of Cain and Abel. You have Abel, who was sacrificing to the Lord with genuine faith and love. *Pure intentions*. But Cain, he saw Abel as competition for God's attention. So instead of laying out his sacrifices in love and faith, as Abel had, Cain did it out of envy and jealousy of his brother. On the surface, you could have put both Cain and Abel's goods side by side and not be able to distinguish between the two. But God *can*. You see, God sees into your heart, and knows your true intentions. Even your *energy*! You have to do things with good intentions. It's ok to mean well and then fail. We are human. That happens. But people tend to think it's strictly what they do and not the reasoning behind it that matters. Or simply the "results". That's hogwash. (*chuckles*). I just said hogwash in church, didn't I…"

The congregation let out a laugh of their own.

The pastor would go on to discuss how, when you put someone who is hiding something in the light long enough, the darkness eventually draws itself out because it can no longer handle the light. You could have someone who pretends to be someone that they are not, and for a while the facade holds, but sooner or later, the mask will fall and the truth will come out. The lesson is that it is much easier to tell the truth the first time before the truth tells itself later down the road at the most inconvenient of times. If only I knew how many times that advice could have helped me in the past. I sometimes get the feeling that Shannon is not really who she makes herself out to be, but she also hasn't given a clear indicator as to what her actual intentions are either. Since it has been of no *immediate* threat, all we can do is wait in nervous suspense. Even with the information Randy was able to provide to me, she has never actually acted on any of the threats she has made to anyone. She just seems to be an expert manipulator and likes to intimidate people.

I am still feeling guilty for betraying Hailey in New York, even though I was blackmailed into it. Shannon more or less raped me. Her threats of retribution, especially as it affected things at a national scale, robbed me of any ability I had to express my lack of consent, and I gave in so that I could simply get it over with and keep AURORA's mission from going awry. It didn't help matters that I actually got some sort of curious fulfillment out of the experience… mostly because of how I was fantasizing about her the first few months after I met her. But now that it has passed, I feel a level of anger towards the situation. Might as well change my name from Shane to "Shame". Now if Hailey and I at some point *do* go all the way, I will be mentally gauging that experience based on my time with Shannon, which is not fair to her at all. She will already have a hard enough time being comfortable with sex because of her experience with Bergeron, so I always tread lightly around the subject. I don't want to make it any harder on her. The best thing I can try to do is to put it out of mind, but it is like trying a potent drug, and though I haven't had it since, sometimes it's all I can think about. Comes to show that when one little thing is allowed to compromise your integrity, it's a downward spiral from there. For everyone. Whenever I pass by a mirror, I do the world a favor and look away. It is an unpleasant reminder of how my former innocence has become defiled.

*[Queue song "Dubioza Kolektiv – No Escape (From Balkan)"]*

*(3 days earlier - Point of view of Chip at a local bar)*

Nineteen year-old Chip Howard made his way into a busy bar in the next town over. Chip remains the 'nerd' of Trent and Rico's in-crowd, still the butt of all their jokes. The latest of these was that he is the final one in the posse to have never gotten laid. One by one he was always turned down by those he asked. At one point he even worked up the courage to ask Lynn just so he could get it over with, but she waited until they were in front of a large group of people in public before laying out her brutal and humiliating rejection of him. Even Brent lost his V-card. Chip came close to resigning from the League of Enlightenment. But as always, having nowhere else to go, he remained with the group and just took the hit.

As Chip walked through the door, he noticed that the guy checking the IDs, a tall man in his late 20s, was not paying attention to the door and had his focus directed somewhere behind him. Without hesitation, Chip swung around the corner and on the other side of the rope so that it appeared that he had already checked in. *Success*! He was able to get to the bar table and have a seat. He looked over to a young man sitting to his right, who appeared to be taking a swig of Coke. The guy's left hand had a purple, circular stamp on it, likely indicating that he was underage. Chip managed to sneak by without the stamp, so it would appear he was of age. He looked forward again as the bartender began to approach him from the left. Eye contact was made as he slowly formed a grin on his face. Chip adjusted his glasses as the bartender stopped in front of him.

"Let me guess..." The bartender started. He was about 5'9" with dark brown hair. A condescending smirk spread across his face. "Can't score a chick to save your life?"

"Yeah, you can say that..." Chip said. Initially, he had no intent of giving him eye contact, nor having a conversation. He just was trying to have a day out to clear his head and was not in the mood for small talk. "I'll take an import."

"Coming up," the bartender said, turning around and fetching a beer from the cooler. He turned back around, popped the cap underneath the table and set it in front of Chip. Chip grabbed the beer and took a swig, still gazing forward and appearing to be spaced out.

"How did you know?" Chip asked.

The bartender paused, his smirk returning. He looked at Chip as if he were staring into his soul. "Let's just say… intuition."

Chip nodded his head and proceeded to make a quick analysis of his surroundings, taking a glance to his left, behind him, and then to the right before facing forward again.

"Honestly, man. Girls are nothing but trouble." The bartender continued. Chip finally looked over and read the name "Mitch" on his nametag. Mitch continued talking. "I just go out and lay 'em. Hit em' and quit em', I hear it said. Better off renting them bitches."

"You're telling me…" Chip said in agreement, taking another swig. As the bottom of the bottle hit the counter, he finally made eye contact. "I have to find other things to do with my time because I can't even find anything on the damn computer let alone in real life."

Mitch laughed. "You don't know where to look?!" he asked. He rested his right wrist on the bar table, facing in Chip's direction and leaning in. "I can teach you what to skip and what to look for."

Chip paused for a moment. *A researcher?* "How much do you know about computers?" he asked.

"I hack up that shit all day long." Mitch said with a grin. He made no effort to hide his gloating, easing in a little closer with almost a whisper of a voice. "All night long too."

'*I might have use for this guy.*' Chip thought. He then spoke up. "So, that means you can hack the government and the colleges and so forth?"

Mitch nodded, returning back to his previous pose. "I did it before and I can do it again."

"Great!" Chip said. *He did it before, he says.* Not only can he, but he also has experience. "I have some *friends* I'd like you to meet. By the way, I'm Chip."

He leaned forward and they shook hands.

"You already know my name because of my tag." Mitch said, now easing back to be completely behind the bar table. "But yeah, I'm Mitch, in case it really wasn't that obvious."

"We call our group the 'League of Enlightenment.'" Chip said, clearing his throat in preparation for reciting the motto. There was a dramatic flair in his presentation. "Licentia praevalet: Anarchy prevails."

Mitch nodded his head. One eye squinted in curiosity. "Sounds good to me." he said. "Who do I meet to join this 'league'?"

"I can introduce you to my superiors." Chip said. "Trent and Rico are their names."

Mitch nodded again. "We can meet them later. But for now I have to do my job. What would you like? (Leans in briefly) And I'm not talking about drinks."

"I would like to find a hot girl to get laid by because I don't wanna stay a virgin my whole life." Chip said. He looked down in embarrassment, although not nearly as shy as one might imagine. "Never seemed to be able to get lucky. One-hundred percent return on rejection."

Mitch glared at him with his best *you're kidding me* face. "I know exactly what you need." He said calmly, trying not to laugh. He felt a level of pity for Chip. "All the other workers had the opportunity to push the red button on their shifts for their patrons. *You* have the honor of being my first."

Mitch reached under the counter and pushed a small red button that was intentionally concealed from view of the bar patrons. The market for sex workers skyrocketed over the past two decades, and people could pretty much order a one night stand in the same way as they could order a shot of whiskey. The odds of finding someone in the bar scene that *wasn't* into casual sex, or someone who wasn't actively cheating on their significant other, assuming they shared the common definition of what "cheating" constituted, was close to zero. Regulars had requested the "Red Button Treatment" at least once during their patronage. As for anyone else, particularly those whose lifestyles clashed with this view on sexuality, they simply had no business in the bar or club scene at all and were encouraged to avoid it. The culture of the 2040s was hostile to non-conformists of all types, and this was certainly no exception. This radical change over the years was what gave Pablo the idea to make a "safe" bar in his basement that reflected the former social atmosphere of that environment, but without the clique expectations or conformity.

"What's that supposed to do?" Chip asked curiously.

Mitch grinned. "You'll find out soon enough."

Chip turned around in his stool and he nearly dropped his beer at the sight. Three scantily dressed girls in their mid-20s, a blonde, a brunette, and a redhead, all closed in on him from different directions, boxing him into the center of a triangle whose sides were their bodies.

All three of the women were wearing tight fitting two pieces that contrasted their physique and hair color. The blonde, with shoulder length hair, was wearing red. The brunette, whose hair was slightly shorter, wore black, and the redhead, who had the longest hair of the three, was wearing a Poison Ivy green. The three women proceeded to take their tops off, shaking their bare breasts at Chip and making kissing motions to him. They put their hands on him as well as each other, as if this were a choreographed performance. Chip didn't know what to do but to submit.

Mitch began to laugh, leaning lazily against the bar table. "This one's on me, ladies. Have fun." He said, waving and then disposing of the remainder of Chip's beer.

"Woo! Get it!" One of the other bar patrons shouted from across the room, with a few others lightly clapping their hands. Many of those present didn't seem fazed at the scene, as it was probably a nightly occurrence. But there were also those who stopped their conversations and looked onward as these scenarios unfolded, looking to offer their encouragement of any "mischief" that was taking place. The girls escorted Chip into one of the back rooms.

About 30 minutes later, Chip returned with a grin on his face. He sat back in the stool, it spinning slightly from the impact of him landing in it. He turned around to see all three girls walking into another room, each looking at him with a smile and waving at him. He waved back.

Mitch looked at Chip with a grin as he returned his gaze forward. "Well? You didn't jizz before you even got in there, did you? Because they looked way too hot for a guy like you."

"No, actually I just had the time of my life." Chip admitted, laughing. "Those three girls were hotter than fire!" He pointed for another beer and Mitch popped the cap before handing one to him.

“I told you!” Mitch said, distributing drinks behind the counter to another patron without even glancing over. “Know where to look. Know who to ask.”

Chip laughed victoriously. No longer was he going to be teased by the League for his lack of… prowess. But telling them how it happened without being called a liar was going to be another challenge.

“I’m out in 20 minutes.” Mitch said, looking at the clock and looking back. “Maybe you can ‘show me to your leader’, or ‘leaders’ if you will, after I clock out?”

“We can do that.” Chip said, taking a swig of his drink. “I’ll have to see if they’re available though. It is getting rather late.”

“So, tell me some background.” Mitch inquired, folding his hands in front of him as if he were prepared to interrogate Chip.

“About me or the League?” Chip asked.

“Both.” Mitch demanded. A slight smile formed on his face that made it clear he was digging for information.

“Well, I am pretty much a simple person.” Chip said. “But I take what I can get. I can catch on to technical things rather quickly. I’m a schemer.”

Mitch nodded in acknowledgment. This got his wheels turning, but Chip was too busy talking to sense this.

“The League was created last year when we went to try and snipe the sitting president.” Chip continued. “It failed because some ex-classmates of mine from school managed to catch on to us.”

“Ok, let me get this straight.” Mitch said, leaning forward and cutting Chip off abruptly. “You guys were trying to cap the president?”

Chip nodded.

Mitch grinned. “Damn, so that sniper that was on the loose in New York, that was you guys?” he asked, easing back into normal position again. His words oozed with envy.

"The sniper is Rico's uncle" Chip said. "Or… was. He ended up a casualty by order of the National Guard, who ended up taking us away for a while. Evidently our adversaries have an enemy of the state helping them, and she was the one that fired on him."

Mitch nodded his head. He smirked. "Do you know her name?"

Chip shook his head no. "I have no clue." he said. "She was about 5'7", shoulder length black hair. Damn hot. Probably way out of my league."

Mitch smiled. "Before we continue, can I get your measurements of height in metric from now on?" he asked. "Old English Imperial makes me wanna barf."

Chip grinned and then cleared his throat. "Ok…" he muttered. He began working out the calculations in his head. "So 5'7" is about 170 cm. Sorry, society's transition from Imperial to Metric is almost complete. Height is one of the last things to go."

"Yeah they better make it quick…" Mitch continued. Something was on his mind but he chose to keep talking. "I may know who you were talking about, but we'll come back to that later. Tell me more about this *League*."

"We are on standby at the moment." Chip said. "Since our sponsor is Trent's dad, Officer Reginald Bergeron of Winchester, he is overseeing operations at the high level and suggested we lay low until his say so. Thank Adolf that he has the pull that he does, otherwise we would still be prisoners."

Mitch laughed. "Thank Adolf… that's a good one. What a sense of humor."

"That ain't shit." Chip said, laughing.

Mitch poured a drink for another nearby patron while continuing to talk. "Believe it or not, I am *somewhat* acquainted with Bergeron." he said. "I used to serve the man donuts before he just flat out disappeared. I was told that he got a promotion."

"He's doing things now that not even I can talk about." Chip continued. "Inside secrecy and all. I am just glad he bailed us out and blackmailed the military into letting us go free."

Mitch nodded. "Tell me about your adversaries." He inquired. He appeared to be tallying checks on the computer. "Make it quick, though."

"I'll profile them." Chip started. "Shane Conliffe. He is kind of short, about 5 foot… er… I mean… 158 cm. Rather arrogant and is rarely anywhere alone. Has a girl named Hailey Burnett attached to his hip at almost all times. He's got dark brown hair. She's a sandy blonde and about 165 cm."

Mitch nodded. "A couple…" he muttered, putting his hand to his chin as if he were deep in thought. "One would make a good bargaining chip against the other at some point."

"We'll keep that in mind…" Chip continued. "I will also mention that, apparently, Shane's dad was killed back in '39 because Bergeron hired a hit out on him. I doubt he knows the details, though. And I also heard that Bergeron raped Hailey."

Mitch nodded. He was taking mental notes but had nothing to say in response to this information.

"We also had a defect." Chip said. "This girl named Maria abandoned us right before we formed the League and was taken in by that guy whose name I keep seeing in the sports section of the news… but I can't for the life of me remember him. But Maria is to be taken in if she is seen because she holds vital information about the Bergerons that can be used against us."

He was talking about no one other than Pablo D'Alvarez.

"That's ok…" Mitch said. He was anxiously digging for more information. "And I am sure we can figure that out later. Any others?"

"Veronica Nolan." Chip said. "She and her boyfriend Gary seem to be pretty good at eluding us, but I think she would have a motive against us as we killed her friend Shamaya almost a year ago."

Mitch nodded his head. "So, about that girl…" he started. "The enemy of the state, I mean. If she is the person I think she is, we may have a secret weapon."

"Really?" Chip asked, taking a swig of his beer and then folding his hands in front of him. "Do tell!"

"Not here…" Mitch said, holding his hand out to halt the conversation. "This is something I would rather discuss in private. The details are too… classified."

"Right on…" Chip continued. He finished his beer and looked on either side of him. Mitch handed him his bill and he signed it. It would automatically charge his credit account.

"Ready to go?" Mitch asked. He looked to be preparing to clock out.

"Let's do it!" Chip said, standing up.

"So, to be clear, you're on *my* team now." Mitch assured. "Let's say we promote you from being the dork in GYM class to someone who actually has a say in things… and then we can make both Trent and Rico *our* bitches for once. Kapeesh?"

Chip nodded his head and smiled. "I'm all in." he said. "Any of this is better than what they have to offer me."

"And don't worry about them finding out about our alliance." Mitch continued. "When the time comes, I will keep you on a separate work shift from them. I am keeping them two together to give them the illusion of control. But it will be just you and I when you work."

The two shook hands in agreement. The proverbial dotted line had been signed by Chip. "Let's take you to meet Trent and Rico." he said.

# CHAPTER 2

# True Colors

[August 23, 2045]

*CONLIFFE, SHANE R. --APPROVED.*

I made my way into HQ. Shannon had messaged my WCD earlier today to help her test a program that she was writing that would allow HQ to be controlled from a remote location. Why she needed *me* to do this was anybody's guess. When I walked in, I was hoping that someone else would be here as well, but it looked like it was between shifts for whoever the second person was supposed to be. Shannon and I had only been in HQ alone a handful of times since returning from New York, and I made every intention of keeping each interaction short. At one point she attempted to seduce me, and she actually listened to me when I told her to stop. But it may have been because we both knew at the time that my mom was on her way to HQ and that she could have walked in on us. Thankfully, she thought better of it.

"I thought Hailey was supposed to be here too." I said, as I approached Shannon at her desk. I really wanted a third party to be present in the room with us.

"She will be." Shannon said, as she picked up her tablet and was swiping at something. "But not until a little bit later. She was helping her parents with one of their landscaping jobs."

I nodded my head. "Gotcha…" I observed her looking over at her monitor and back to the tablet again. "So what's this about being able to control HQ remotely?"

"Yes…" Shannon started. She moved her desk chair over slightly as if to make room for me. "Pull up a seat."

*Sure, why not*? I thought. I pulled the seat from the second desk and rolled it near Shannon's. She proceeded to turn her screen and put me in view of her tablet.

"So the idea is that I made this interface…" Shannon started, moving her hands as she spoke. "It works sort of like a VPN tunnel, but even more secure. So the credentials are two factor authentications with a valid WCD chosen by the username, with two passwords. The first one is to get through the servers in the back and the second one is to remote into whichever computer here that you wish."

My hands were idle and resting in my lap. "So, what do you want me to do?" I asked.

Shannon handed me the tablet. "So I am going to first shut both of these computers down…" she said, as she shut her machine down. "I have the remote wake set. Obviously we can't shut down the backend servers in the other rooms or none of this will work. What I want you to do is to try to remotely start both machines and see if you can remotely access them from the tablet."

"So is this going to go to my WCD?" I asked. I think I understand what she is talking about, but this felt more like a training exercise than me actually assisting her with something. These felt like tasks that she could have done without me, and that she just wanted me here because of the obvious reasons. I would rather be getting some fresh air at the park.

"Yes." Shannon said. "I have already registered your WCD. So you just use the same credentials as if you were on shift on the other computer, and tap your WCD to verify the login."

I proceeded to do this with both machines with ease. "Ok, now what?" I asked.

"Now we wait…" Shannon said. "It may take a moment for the tablet to build your remote profile. (Pause) Want something from the fridge while you wait?"

"Yeah, sure." I said. I could definitely use something to drink. It was the dog days of summer after all.

"I'll get you some lemonade." she said, getting up to go to the kitchen area. "Let me know if anything shows on the tablet."

"Will do…" I said. Everything was loading, albeit slowly. "Is it going to be this slow every time?" I asked.

"Only on the first boot." Shannon said. She made her way to me with my glass of lemonade. "After that your profile should remain in cached memory. Just don't wipe the memory unless you have time for it to recache."

"Thank you…" I said, gently taking the glass from her and drinking the entire glass in one sitting. She gave me a funny look. "What? I was thirsty!"

"Looks like it…" she said, half grinning. She proceeded to take the empty glass from me and set it in the sink. As she made her way back to me, she sort of strutted as if to get my attention.

I sighed in annoyance. "Not gonna work, Shannon…" I said. "I really wish you would stop."

"Oh, you're no fun." she said under her breath, as she sat back in her seat. "How's the program coming along?"

I was able to move the cursor with my finger. I looked over at the other desk and saw the cursor moving in sync with the tablet screen. "So, I see it is using our internal wireless network…" I said, practicing the opening and closing of programs from the tablet. "How does it work outside of HQ?"

"It runs on the same network as the WCDs…" Shannon said. "So as long as those work, so should this."

I nodded my head. "At what point do you think we will have to do this?" I asked.

"Have you seen our roster?" Shannon asked. "It's hard enough to keep people other than me in HQ. Eventually we will have the need to do everything unmanned. You guys could do this from the comfort of your own homes if you wanted. It would solve the problem of people being in the same room that don't get along with each other."

I thought for a moment. This would actually solve our staffing problems. "But what if…" I started to feel a bit heavy headed all of a sudden. *Maybe it's just a momentary fluke*, I thought. My words returned almost as quickly as I lost them. "If someone tries to hack it, how many attempts does it allow for incorrect passwords?"

"After ten unsuccessful tries, the tablet will wipe itself clean." Shannon explained. "And the only restore image is located here on base. Plus, it will take a picture with the camera on each attempt and send it to the WCDs of the senior staff, which is Mr. McFarlane, Pablo, and I. Also any of these two computers that are actively booted will get an alert."

I nodded my head. Whatever this *heavy headed* feeling was didn't seem to be going away. I set the tablet in my lap and began to hold my palm to my head. Things were starting to get a little fuzzy.

"Are you alright, Shane?" Shannon asked, an eyebrow raised. She had a suspicious expression on her face.

"I… feel weird…" I muttered. I was seeing stars and my breath felt cold. "Dizzy."

"Here, let me help you to the couch." Shannon said, rushing to my side and pulling me up by my underarms. The tablet fell to the ground, but was saved by its leather casing. As I was on my feet I was feeling tingly everywhere. Something wasn't right. I was beginning to wonder if she put something in my drink, but I could neither think clearly nor put my thoughts to words.

"That… lemonade…" I managed to mutter.

Shannon laid me on the couch that was against the wall. A sly sneer formed on her face. "Ahh yes, you finally caught on." she said. She proceeded to undress in front of me. "Consider this a special early birthday present. From me… to you."

Tomorrow is my 18th birthday.

*[Queue song: Sonic Youth - Teenage Riot - Intro only]*

*Oh no she didn't*, I thought. But I was powerless to stop her. I could not summon any strength to act upon my own free will. I was powerless as I felt myself fading away, but was painfully aware of what was taking place. Clearly she spiked my drink with something not unlike a date rape drug. Where she could have gotten something like that was anybody's guess. *I hope Hailey busts her ass*, I thought. Surely she would have left evidence out somewhere. I had no way of finding out in this state. All I could do now was let Shannon use me like a glorified sex toy. *The lack of conscience in this woman.* I was so loopy that I hardly noticed that Shannon had already undressed my bottom half and was preparing to get on top of me. It felt like one of those dreams where you were pinned down and paralyzed while some presence from the astral realm proceeded to have their way with you. Like sleep paralysis.

Except this was happening in the flesh. As I saw Shannon's devious smile drawing closer to my face, everything went black.

-------45-Minutes-Later------

*BURNETT, HAILEY S. --APPROVED.*

Hailey made her way into HQ in order to begin her shift. Shannon remained at her desk pretending not to notice. As Hailey approached her desk, she stopped at the sight of Shane crashed asleep on the couch.

"What is *he* doing here?" she asked, pointing over at Shane on the couch. "And why is he asleep?"

Shannon finally looked up from her work, looking over at Shane and then to Hailey. "He was helping me test a device. After which he got tired. So he crashed here."

Hailey gave Shannon her *Pisces Eyes* as there was a silent contest between them. Then she broke the silence. "Yeah… the device between your legs…" she said. She then approached Shannon and got in her face. "WHAT DID YOU DO TO HIM?"

Shannon smirked confidently, not having even flinched from Hailey's proximity. "I told you. Testing my device." She said, pointing at the tablet that Shane was using, except it was sitting upright between her right monitor and the right sidewall of her desk.

"Your device?" Hailey asked. Her voice grew more intense. "YOUR device? After what happened in New York, I highly doubt he did this willingly."

She looked back over at the kitchen area and noticed the empty glass that served Shane's lemonade earlier that afternoon. Then she spotted a suspicious looking bottle near the end of the counter. "You… you *drugged* him?"

In a sudden movement, Shannon grabbed Hailey by the front of her shirt and grit her teeth, her eyes growing a lifeless black. She stood to her feet. "If word of this ventures outside of these walls, there *will* be a reckoning! I will *gut you* like the fish you are!"

Hailey seemed unfazed by the reference to her zodiac sign. "You *cannot* have him, Shannon!" she said. "Believe me, in due time it is *you* that will receive your end of this *reckoning*."

Shannon smirked, still having Hailey's shirt in her grip. "I already *had* him." she said calmly. "*Twice now*, in fact. Why don't you walk over there and check on him? (Smiles playfully) I betcha he still smells like me!"

Hailey went to raise her fist, but then Shannon grabbed her arm using her free hand. "Na-ah, I wouldn't do that!" Shannon said, releasing the hand from Hailey's shirt and pulling out a blackout syringe. Her eyes went back to being black again. "One misstep and I will knock you out, and when you come to, you will wish you were *dead*!"

Hailey's jaw dropped in horror. Whatever confidence and bravery she had was shattered. "I… I knew I had bad vibes about you but… this is over the top, Shannon!" she cried out. "You are so much more… *evil* than I gave you credit for. Talk about uncomfortable working conditions…"

Shannon tilted her head tauntingly, her grip on Hailey's arm tightening to a point where it would cause Hailey pain if she tried to fight. "What are you going to do?" she taunted. "Take it up with Mr. McFarlane? He is in the dark like everyone else. And when the couch hottie comes to, he won't remember a thing!"

"How *DARE* you!" Hailey screamed in anger. "They *trusted* you! Tell me, did you have *anything* to do with what happened to Randy and Shamaya? I bet you *did*, didn't you?"

Shannon calmly sighed. "You already know too much." she said. Quickly and without warning, she stabbed Hailey in the arm and injected the contents of the syringe. She raised her voice slightly. "I can't trust you to keep your mouth shut. So it's sleepy time for you."

After the injection, Shannon shoved Hailey against the side of one of the couches with both hands as if to wear her down. Hailey was still on her two feet, but leaning against the couch and looking to be losing strength. She eyed Shannon with despair, but shook her head as if to give a dire warning. Her breathing grew labored. "You… all it'll take… one missed step… and you'll *stumble*…"

Shannon set the spent syringe on her desk and turned back to Hailey. "*If* that ever happens…" she said confidently. "*Which it won't*! You won't be here to see it. I had Randy cornered in fear. He grew resistant to these syringes due to how often I had to use them on him. He was ready to blow the whistle, so I put him away."

With her energy almost depleted, Hailey gave Shannon a look of surprise. "Your tears… the crying… it was…"

"An act, yes…" Shannon nodded in a gaze of insincere empathy. "Regrettably so. I can turn those things on and off on demand as if I flipped a switch. (Points at self) I'm the Mistress of Manipulation. Now, why don't you be a good girl and go to sleep already? Next to your *boyfriend*. Won't that be so… (Smiles deviously) Sweet?"

"Fuck you…" Hailey snarled. The effects of the syringe were beginning to take over.

Shannon folded her arms in front of her. "I would…" she said. Then she taunted her with a smile. "But Shane curbed my needs for the time being. Thanks for the offer, though!"

Hailey groaned and stepped forward, raising her right fist as if intending to punch Shannon, but she did not have the strength to let it fly. She collapsed in a heap on the floor.

Shannon laughed out loud. "Yes…" she said, reaching down to pull Hailey onto a couch. "Sleep, darling. Sleep!"

Hailey's eyes finally closed. She was out cold. Shannon was surprised that Hailey was able to stand for as long as she did with the effects of the syringe, but it only mattered to her that she succumbed. Neither Shane nor Hailey would remember what led to either of them crashing, giving Shannon ample time to dispose of her evidence and to ensure that the world would keep on spinning when they woke up.

# CHAPTER 3

# No Good Deed Goes Unpunished

*(The next day, police headquarters)*

"Officer Bergeron!"

A female attendant in heels quickly approached him from the opposite direction as he was walking in the hallway. The 9am-6pm business hours had begun not more than an hour earlier. The 1st floor was where the isolation ward and all of the cells were located, but the 2nd floor was where all of the offices and the staff were. As always, today was a busy day in the office. Officer Bergeron has had his hands full trying to find ways to keep a stranglehold on the community since Barr became president.

"What is it?" Bergeron asked in an annoyed tone. The woman stopped in front of him holding a datapad.

"Well, if you're too busy I won't bother you, chief." she responded in a passive-aggressive tone and handed the datapad over to Bergeron. "But I think this is something you'd be interested in."

Bergeron backed up a step and put one hand in his pocket, the other taking the datapad from the woman's hands.

"Gerald Cantrell has a proposal." she continued. "He would like to organize a meeting with you as soon as possible."

Bergeron nodded his head as he analyzed the information on the tablet. "Thanks, you're dismissed." he said. The woman turned around and walked off as he turned the other direction and made his way to the office. He shut the door behind him as he entered and went to his desk, connecting the datapad to a docking stand that illuminated everything on two monitors and enabled external controls such as a keyboard and a mouse. The screens came to life as the report that was on the screen of the datapad was transferred to the monitors. He began to look it over. Cantrell proposed that since President Barr was having a difficult time reversing the Enemy of the State law at the congressional level that they buy up billboards in the area with a slideshow of known Enemies of the State, and post rewards for each of their findings. *Why not do this nationwide?* Bergeron thought. He picked up his desk phone and paged a couple of other officers. "Turley. Rodney. Conference room 2. You have fifteen minutes."

He set the receiver down and disconnected the tablet from the docking station. In a rushed fashion, he made his way out of his office and to the conference room to prepare for the meeting. As he reached the door, Officer Turley was already at the door waiting for him.

"What is this about?" he asked curiously.

As Turley finished his sentence, Officer Rodney made his way to them. He stopped in front of them and glanced back and forth between them.

"I have a project for you two following this meeting." Bergeron stated. Without looking away from them, he reached his free hand behind him to crack open the door. As the door creaked open, he pointed toward the doorway to the conference room with both hands. "Entrė Vu." he said.

Turley and Rodney entered the conference room with Bergeron following behind. The lights kicked on from the motion sensor of their entry as they went to sit down. The room was big enough to seat six, with two on each side of the table and one on each end. Bergeron sat on the end across from the door and Turley and Rodney sat on opposite sides. Bergeron mounted the tablet on a dock that was in front of him and a projector kicked on in front of him to show the screen on the wall.

"Gerald Cantrell plans on funding a program to buy up billboards and post slideshows of enemies of the state in the area." He explained. "Your job will be to oversee the project in *our* community and that it gets implemented."

"How are we supposed to do that?" Rodney asked.

"Let's leave that to *the man*." Bergeron stated, tapping the tablet to call Gerald.

<BEEP!><BEEP!>

"Bergeron. Thank you for your prompt response. There is a matter of urgency to discuss."

"Let's get started." Bergeron replied eagerly, positioning himself comfortably in his seat and folding his hands in front of him.

"I am sending you a file of all the billboards I plan on purchasing and programming to display slideshows of all known local enemies of the state."

"Alright, ready to receive." Bergeron said, turning to his computer to confirm a command.

"There is another thing..." Gerald continued. "My son came bearing a message, and it is as follows: *You guys better find some shelter! There's a big ol' storm coming!*"

Bergeron looked back up at the screen and smiled. "Excellent." he said, once again folding his hands in front of him. "So Miss Boyer has accepted her plea for freedom then."

Gerald nodded. "That is correct." he said. "Mitch saw her in New York walking with a young man who barely looked out of high school. But they had met beforehand to discuss the terms not long after your town's protest rally two years ago."

Bergeron continued. "It is my understanding that Miss Boyer, if she succeeds in eliminating all members of this *AURORA* organization, that she will not only turn their base over to me, but she will be granted her freedom and no longer be an enemy of the state."

"Correct." Gerald said. "While my company suffered from her actions, President Barr and that organization are a bigger threat. I say that for now, we keep things as they are. Bide our time and let her stir some chaos. She will continue to *pose* as an enemy of the state. Go ahead and put her on the billboards, but it is intended to be a diversion. So long as she is following along with our agenda, she will be allowed her freedom."

"She seems to have wasted no time." Bergeron continued. "Everything is going exactly according to plan. She has already eliminated Randy Morris, and I had my son Trent take out Shamaya Tolbert because it was determined that she was immune to the effects of the blackout syringes. She had overheard a conversation last fall that was not hers to hear and survived a few more days than she should have."

"So that's two down already…" Gerald said. "How many are left?"

"Other than Shannon herself, not many." Bergeron said. He pulled up a list on his computer. "I will send you the list. But I have to ask. Trent reported that Shannon was allowed to kill the would-be assassin. Why is that?"

"Lucas was expendable." Gerald said. "I also struck a deal with an associate of a New York strip club who wanted Lucas eliminated so she could take over his business. The man needed too much guidance from others to make a move. These tasks require individuals who have the ability to be *autonomous*. Besides, it was a commendable display to force Miss Boyer's *friends* into trusting her."

It was not unusual for business and law enforcement to work together and use people as bait or fodder to accomplish their goals.

"Here is another interesting factor…" Bergeron continued. "When I got my hands on her four years ago, she was driving a 2005 Honda Civic with a forged registration. My colleagues hardwired a black box to that car after she was arrested in the event that the car was to be tampered with."

Officer Rodney spoke up. "Turns out that car was taken to an after-hours black market before their trip to New York."

Gerald nodded. "Firearm purchases, no doubt."

"That's what we suspect…" Bergeron said. "Shannon has kept her fair share of secrets from us too. But even if she is following her *own* agenda, so long as she doesn't interfere with ours, I am fine with whatever she does. And so far, she has fallen right in line."

"Keep a close eye on her…" Gerald continued. "But I have reason to believe that she wants her freedom bad enough that she is going to do whatever it takes to secure it. When she first joined their program, she genuinely *was* on board with them. So most think she still is. Since Mitch met with her, she has brilliantly spaced out incidents all the while continuing to play the part that she always has. However, there is going to come a point where she will have to drop her mask, and I think that point is approaching *very* soon."

"I agree…" Bergeron said. "One of my son's associates was acquainted with Mitch a few days ago. So not only are you and I putting our heads together, but so are they. We will combine forces to make sure that AURORA is taken down."

"The next thing I need you to do is connect with other law enforcement agencies around the country." Gerald requested. "Round up a list of enemies of the state. Make sure the billboards are made geographically relevant. Each suspect is to be shown on boards within a 100km radius of their last known sighting. Offer a reward for every enemy of the state caught. However, Shannon is a special case. Though she knows that no danger will come to her if she is *caught* by anyone, since the reward can only be given one time, she too will have to remain hidden for the time being so that she doesn't blow her cover by getting caught more than once."

"Not a problem." Bergeron continued enthusiastically. "And so long as I keep pulling the strings at town hall, this will be the perfect economic opportunity for those who wish to pay their debts. Why go out and do the monkey work when we can have the desperate public go out and do it for us?"

"Like a conscripted police force." Turley commented.

"That just might work." Gerald said. "Let's continue our espionage for now, but I have a feeling that if Shannon hasn't already hit the accelerator on this project, Mitch will. Our pieces are going to fall in place so fast that they will be blindsided. Checkmate is on the horizon."

(*Point of view - Pablo - September 7, 2045)*

"So, yeah, we've got one hell of a game to play tomorrow night."

Pablo sat on the couch in his basement with a small Bluetooth speaker on the end table playing old school hip-hop and smoking a joint. Maria was at his side. Recently she applied to the university that Pablo was attending, but got accepted on probation. It was better than nothing, however, and she was taking what she could get. She also tried her hand at baseball when Pablo discovered that she had a hell of a throwing arm. During this decade, sports was becoming more diversified in that gender barriers were beginning to be broken in one profession after another. She ended up being the first female to play baseball at the university with the collegiate baseball league. Though she was a benchwarmer much of the time, she did end up playing relief when called upon, particularly as a shortstop.

"I can't believe I threw that error to first base…" Maria muttered, putting her head down. Pablo handed her the joint and she took a puff of it. "I should've known better to hesitate when I have a runner heading from first to second."

She took a 2nd hit as Pablo continued. "Actually, you should always try to get the lead runner out first." he suggested. "The ones closer to scoring position are the bigger threats."

"Coach yelled at me when I did that the last time." Maria continued. She handed Pablo the joint back.

"Well, the coach is smart, but I've earned enough trust where he don't question my motives." Pablo said. He took a hit and continued. "Besides, everybody makes mistakes. You have to build that muscle memory, and that takes practice."

"What about the double play?" Maria asked.

"Exactly why you throw the leading runner out first." Pablo said. He took his 2nd hit. "Throw to 2nd and *they*'ll throw it to 1st. There's your double play right there."

<BEEP!><BEEP!>

Pablo looked at his WCD. It was Mr. McFarlane. "Hold on, let me take this." he said. He handed the joint to Maria and answered the call. "Pablo speaking."

"Pablo, have you heard from Shannon? I have something critical to discuss with her and she isn't answering the main line or her WCD. Neither is Hailey."

Pablo looked over at Maria, who had a deer in headlights look, and then looked back at his WCD. "I haven't. Does Shane know anything?"

"Shane's at home." Mr. McFarlane said. "I had him try calling them too and he can't reach them either. He is worried sick that one of them may have snapped at each other and the worst happened. Might you back him up?"

"So what are you suggesting?" Pablo asked. This *is* suspicious, he thought.

"Pick Shane up and head over to HQ. Shannon needs to know that her face is popping up on wanted ads on billboards nationwide. I just saw one off of I-64. And I'm three states away."

Pablo paused in horror. There was about five seconds of silence before he could speak. "So, they have expanded the enemy of the state program? But how? Wasn't Barr supposed to get rid of that?"

"President Barr has done his job as president… a little too well. He has gotten the Federal Government out of a lot of affairs that belong to the states. Unfortunately, in doing so he no longer has control over the things he just legislated back to the state and local levels. That includes the networking of state and local law enforcement agencies to offer rewards for the known enemies of the state as an incentive to turn our neighbors into highway patrolmen."

"So we fucked up?" Pablo asked. *This can't be good.*

"I'm afraid so…" Mr. McFarlane continued. "We thought we were trying to do the right thing. Barr is a good man with the right intentions. But he inherited a system whose complexity that all of us alike have underestimated. You can stop the federal government from being too powerful, but it is easier said than done to eliminate the already existing cross-state network, which in reality cannot be legislated out of existence if we are to have a free society."

"What are we going to do for Shannon then?" Pablo asked. "I'm sure she will want to be free at some point."

Mr. McFarlane sighed. "With Bergeron and his cronies still in power in our area, she is not safe there. But because he is collaborating with so many other municipalities, there is nowhere she can move to where they won't be looking for her, now that money is involved. I fear that we have *no* options."

"A presidential pardon?" Pablo asked.

"Unfortunately, that's not feasible." Mr. McFarlane continued. "If we ask him to pardon Shannon, then he would be obligated to pardon everyone else. As president, he can't be biased or have any favorites, if he wants to maintain his integrity. Even for Shannon."

Pablo sighed in frustration. "If it weren't for her, Barr wouldn't have been elected. Doesn't he owe her?"

"The pieces would have fallen as they did with or without Shannon." Mr. McFarlane pointed out. "AURORA is far from being the only underground activist group, and to be quite honest, outside of our intervention in the assassination attempts and the speech writing, our effect individually was minimum. It was the converging and accumulation of activity from everyone around the country that elected him into office. Unity achieved that. We can't take credit for everything."

"Oh, so that's why *she's* on a billboard three states away?" Pablo scoffed.

"Shannon's publicity has nothing to do with AURORA *or* Barr." Mr. McFarlane continued. "That giant medical company is still pissed off at her. She did that on her own. Had nothing to do with us. Also nothing to do with politics. You forget who actually pulls the strings of those in power. We all should have learned something from this. Our politicians are nothing more than scapegoats for the men behind the scenes calling the shots."

## CHAPTER 4

# Interior Issues

It was only a week ago when I was here the last time. The time before that was the day before my birthday, and I had a weird memory lapse. I was helping Shannon test a remote interface on the tablet and then I woke up on the couch. Hailey was there as well and I didn't even remember her entering the room. Something didn't feel right to me for us *both* to be asleep like that. Neither Hailey nor I could put our finger on what was going on, and without concrete evidence that something was fishy, there was nothing we could do but to press on. We couldn't help but to feel as if there was a piece of the puzzle missing. No matter how hard I tried, any moment after I drank the lemonade… *the lemonade*. Maybe that had something to do with it? With any luck, Shannon herself was probably asleep, and with Pablo at my side, if there is anything going on behind the scenes, we were determined to blow the lid right off of it. Initially I thought of the possibility that she and Hailey could have been picked up by law enforcement if they were spotted in Commerce Square or something, thanks to the billboards that Mr. McFarlane was talking about. But I had a hunch that this would not be the case.

Formal meetings in general had been sporadic for the entire team since we all returned from New York, most of it because Mr. McFarlane retired and had gone on a national tour to be a motivational speaker for troubled youth. He was rarely available, let alone in touch with us, and we hadn't received many orders from him lately. There weren't even any plans to recruit anyone. Those of us here were it. While we contributed to the success in getting Barr into office, there was nothing else on the political front to focus on, at least in the near term. That was, until today. The billboard issue was most likely collaborated by Bergeron himself and less likely by my old high school foes.

Trent, Rico and the others were still pretty much off the radar, and even though I suggested being cautious anyway, Mr. McFarlane seems to have put them on the backburner, telling us not to worry about it. Veronica and Gary, although still associated with us to an extent, got an apartment together near the local University where they are attending, and have had their personal affairs at the forefront of their priorities. Both of them are now only part time members. Pablo was the next in line to try to coordinate AURORA activities, but he didn't know much more than the rest of us. Regardless, he did his best. Our job was to keep an eye out as we did before for any evidence of the president's life being threatened (it hadn't been lately), but mainly to keep an eye out for things locally. While nothing had been happening in recent time anyway, the silence was petrifying. We were more likely to have internal issues due to Shannon and Hailey's inability to get along with each other. That was a problem on its own. We tried to get Muhammad to stay at HQ with her to assist, but he insisted on infiltrating the police station instead by posing as an illegal immigrant and getting hired in as a janitor. His intention was to engage in espionage, and having made it decades under the radar like he has, he would be the perfect man for the job.

Muhammad said that it was the most he could do to help and that because of his age, and his disconnect with modern technology, he considered himself expendable. The possibility of death did not seem to scare him at all, and he made it clear to us that he would die for the cause if it came down to it. He just seemed ready to die in general, but wanted to have it be meaningful. Pablo gave him the ok since that was what he wanted, and he went for it. He has worked there for three weeks, and although he has not heard any specifics yet or anything particularly triggering, he is certain there are multiple background operations that sound like they would be of concern to us. Pablo mentioned the billboards reported by Mr. McFarlane and Muhammad said that he had heard chatter about it last week, but hadn't heard about it since. He has since been tasked with trying to orchestrate a list of the districts in which Bergeron has contact with so that we know what cities and towns to blacklist. Given what Hailey's parents told us, I informed Muhammad that Troy Bigelow was trustworthy and that if he needed help with anything internally, he could be of assistance. However, he was also aware that he had to make any efforts in communication as discreet as possible.

Pablo and I parked at Commerce Square and walked from there to HQ. We got to the storm doors and I opened them up for him to walk through first. As I followed behind, I closed them behind me. We both signed in at the door with our hand prints.

*D'ALVAREZ, PABLO F. --APPROVED.*

*CONLIFFE, SHANE R. --APPROVED.*

As we walked in, it was eerily quiet. There were only two lights on in the facility, one above the kitchen sink and one at Shannon's desk. The first thing that caught my eye was that Shannon appeared to be asleep at her desk. She was face down with her head resting on her arms in front of her. As we went to approach her, my heart jumped at what else I saw.

(*gasp*) “Hailey!”

She was crumpled on the floor in front of the couches. Fragments of a shattered liquor bottle littered the perimeter, and it was hard not to notice the bloody welt on Hailey’s head. “Pablo, come here!”

I motioned him to come over and he stopped dead in his tracks at the sight. “No… she didn’t…” he muttered in disbelief.

“Yeah… she did.” I muttered back looking down at Hailey. I bent down and cradled her in my arms to where her head was resting on me. She was breathing, just unconscious. It was a miracle that she appeared to have dodged most of the glass shards during her fall. “Let’s get her on a couch…” I said. The nearest couch, which was the one closest to the hallway, had shards of glass hidden in it. “A… clean couch…”

Since Pablo and I both were wearing decent footwear, we were not worried about stepping on the glass fragments for the moment. He picked her up by her legs while I picked up at her shoulders. We laid her on the couch that was on the opposite wall. He took a few steps back toward Shannon’s desk, but stopped when he noticed that I had not moved from my position of observing Hailey.

“Let’s deal with Shannon first…” Pablo said calmly. “Let Hailey rest for the time being.”

I followed behind Pablo and we stopped directly behind her.

“She’s passed out!” I whispered, pointing at the right side corner of her work desk. There was an open bottle of 80 proof Vodka sitting there. She had her tablet, which showed a lock symbol, off to the right side as well. *At least she locked that*, I thought. The desktop terminal on her desk had put itself to sleep from sitting idle, the screen giving an elapsed time that the machine had been offline. The numbers read 1:59:39 and continued to count up second by second. She must’ve passed out a good two hours ago.

"Well, here goes…" Pablo muttered, shaking his head reluctantly. He violently shook Shannon's shoulder. "Hey. Wake up! Just what in the hell happened here, Shannon?"

She began to move, but slowly and weakly. There was a little bit of a groan as she lifted her head. She appeared unable to lift her head straight up, but it was up enough to where she was able to look up at Pablo and I with glazed, bloodshot eyes. Her hair almost kept its messed up form when she lifted her head.

"Umm… Hi." I said. I wanted to wait for her to show signs of being cognitive before I began questioning her. But Pablo had no such patience.

"You're in deep shit." Pablo said sternly.

"Ohh…. Umm…. Hey…" Shannon said slowly and weakly. She spoke as if she had a sore throat. "How did you…"

Her head almost dropped back on her desk and her palm caught it before it could hit the desk. She was completely wasted. In an effort to try to fight it, she shook her head and pushed herself away from her desk with both hands, moving the desk chair back by about a quarter of a meter or so. Using the desk to prop herself up on her feet, she began standing on her own, but in the moment that she went to take a step, she staggered. She caught herself on the couch that had the glass shards, and proceeded to lean over it and throw up on one of the seat cushions. She was either drunk or hungover.

Pablo glanced at me. "Call Mr. McFarlane." He said, as he approached Shannon from behind to support her.

"Please don't…" Shannon managed to choke out.

"Why shouldn't I?" Pablo snapped angrily. "This has gone on long enough, Shannon! Hailey is injured and I think you owe us some answers!"

Shannon continued to lean over the couch with both of her hands propped against the back. Her breathing was labored from throwing up. "Bitch had it coming…"

Pablo let go of Shannon and backed up about two steps. “Turn around and face me.” he said. Shannon remained in her present position. “NOW!” he commanded.

Shannon turned around and began screaming at Pablo. “I CAN’T FUCKING DO THIS ANYMORE, PABLO! I WANT TO DIE!” she grit her teeth and her eyes went black. “I am mere *seconds* from taking one of those glass shards and slitting my own goddamn throat!”

“You will do no such thing!” Pablo put his hand on his hip confidently and told her. He then turned to me. “Shane, if you would please… the sooner we clean up the mess over here, the better.”

I walked over and proceeded to take the soiled cushions one by one to the kitchen area. There was a portable shop vac under the sink and I proceeded to start cleaning the cushions one by one. The one with the barf needed extra work. I would have to do the actual living room area next, but I was more concerned with what Pablo was dealing with. Not to mention tending to Hailey’s well-being when all of this was said and done. If she were any worse, I would have tended to her first and did the cleanup afterwards.

“From the beginning…” Pablo started, grabbing Shannon’s shoulders. “What happened between you and Hailey?”

Shannon gave Pablo a devilish grin and preceded to head-butt him.

“Ow, God damnit, Shannon!” Pablo shouted, holding his head. Shannon proceeded to make an attempt toward the door but due to her being hung over, she tripped and fell once she crossed the line dividing the kitchen area from the rest of the room.

*Holy shit*! I was in disbelief at what I had just witnessed. I have never seen Shannon do that to Pablo before. She was absolutely unhinged. *Maybe her true colors come out with the alcohol*, I thought. I found myself stunned as I witnessed the spectacle before me. Pablo finally drew his stun gun and used it on Shannon without hesitation. *No wonder he keeps that thing on him at all times*.

"Shane... I need your help..." Pablo said. I stood up at attention prepared to abandon my present task. He continued. "Go into the survival room at the end of the hall. There is a set of restraints. Bring them to me, and then send Mr. McFarlane the following message. *Our worst fears. Phase 2.*"

I nodded and proceeded to make my way down the hall. I heard the conversation as I performed what was asked of me. While I was in the survival room I quickly did a voice to text to Mr. McFarlane with Pablo's message.

"You guys had it in for me all along..." Shannon said. She had a rare panic in her voice. "You *can't* win! It's too late!"

"What are you talking about?" Pablo asked. He gave Shannon a confused but surprised look.

I made my way back down the hall with the restraints, one for the arms and one for the legs. "I suppose that is a question that we should ask Hailey when she wakes up." I said, handing them to Pablo.

Shannon sighed and bit her lip. She was worried about something. Pablo proceeded to restrain her. After she was bound, he reached for her WCD and proceeded to remove it from her wrist. "I guess you won't be needing this anymore..." He said, pocketing the device. "Shannon Jean Boyer, you are hereby terminated from AURORA."

"Ha, that's what you think." Shannon said. She then looked in the direction of the tablet on her desk and raised her voice. "Computer. Activate program *Zero Hour*. Authorization code, Shannon."

*[Queue song: M83 - Don't Save Us From The Flames]*

*AUTHORIZATION --CONFIRMED.* The tablet appeared to recognize the command. A low pitched alarm began emitting from both of the computer desks as if we were on some kind of starship that was screaming "Red Alert".

My heart sank. *This is not happening right now*, I thought. I looked over at Shannon in horror, and she had a devious sneer on her face. I turned to Pablo. "Pablo?"

All I could get out of my mouth was his name, trying to ask him what was going on. But he seemed just as lost as I was. Whatever was happening now was premeditated on both sides. Somewhere along the line a threshold was crossed in regards to the lack of trust we seemed to have for one another as a group. Pablo and Mr. McFarlane appeared to have been suspecting Shannon's treachery since Shamaya's death, and even more so since Randy's. At the same time, Shannon had a contingency plan of her own.

Pablo proceeded to use the stun gun on Shannon once more for good measure to keep her down. "Explain yourself!" he commanded. "What is all this?"

Shannon's expression went from devious to cheerful. "Bergeron and company are homing in on us as we speak!" she said. "Thanks for making me play my Trump card. I have waited *two years* for this!"

Two years? Seems to almost fall in line with the protest rally. Just then, I spotted a suspicious looking black case behind Shannon's computer monitor. *This is odd*, I thought. I reached for it and proceeded to unzip it. *No...*

I held the contents of the case up where Pablo could see it. He did a double take. "Blackout syringes…" he muttered.

"How do you think I got away with this for so long?" Shannon sneered, looking back and forth between us both. "You all just signed your death sentence. In exchange for eliminating *all* of you, I receive my freedom!"

"Shane. Now!" Pablo said urgently. I handed him the case and he proceeded to take one of the syringes out and injected Shannon in the right arm with it. "So that's what this is about. (Pulls syringe back) You are one hell of a rat, you know that?"

"It's too late!" Shannon said. She seemed like she would have been starting to laugh hysterically if the drug had not been coursing through her so fast.

Pablo set the spent syringe on the other computer desk, whose computer was shut down this whole time. He sat at the desk and proceeded to boot up the computer. He tried to sign in. *ACCESS DENIED*. "Fuck!"

Shannon laughed. "I covered my bases, Pablo..." she said. "They will have control of our base of operations soon enough."

"Like hell they will..." Pablo said. He turned to me and pointed at his WCD and then pointed at me. He proceeded to key in a message.

"What do you think you're doing?" Shannon asked. Her voice was getting weaker as the syringe was beginning to take effect.

"You forget..." Pablo started. He briefly pointed at himself. "I play baseball for a living. Covering bases is *my* job."

He sent the message and my WCD buzzed almost immediately. It seemed that he had this message prepared in advance. I felt hopeful that Mr. McFarlane and Pablo thought ahead on this possibility. *But for how long*, I wondered.

*MR. MCFARLANE INTEGRATED AN "ULTIMATE KILL SWITCH" INTO THE SYSTEM THAT WILL BYPASS ALL OTHER FORMS OF SECURITY. THIS IS HOW WE SURVIVED THE MOLE LOCKDOWN IN 2042. SHANNON DOES NOT KNOW ABOUT THIS. ONLY HE AND GEORGE KNEW ABOUT IT. IT HAS BEEN IN THE SYSTEM SINCE THE VERY BEGINNING. WHEN GEORGE DIED, HE ENTRUSTED ME WITH IT. FOLLOW THESE INSTRUCTIONS EXACTLY: SERVER RACK 3. REMOTE IN FROM THE 3RD STATION IN THE HISTORY ROOM. COMMAND PROMPT. TYPE REMOTE SR3. ONCE IN, ENTER KILLSWITCH /U. PIN IS 0665. I WILL CONFIRM ON MY WCD AND THE ENTIRE SYSTEM WILL*

*SHUT DOWN. IT WILL BE DOWN PERMANENTLY UNTIL MR. MCFARLANE REACTIVATES IT WITH A PHYSICAL KEY, WHICH ONLY HE POSSESSES AND HE KEEPS IT ON HIS PERSON. GIVE ME A THUMBS UP WHEN DONE.*

I nodded my head and went into the "history" room. I did exactly as Pablo said and it worked just as he had explained. I watched all the computers around me shut down. When this was done, I got up and quickly checked the other rooms. From what I could tell, the entire system was now locked. I got back into the main room and gave Pablo a thumbs up. The alert sounds had also stopped.

"Perfect…" He said. He looked down at Shannon, who was now unconscious.

"What do we do with her?" I asked. I knew that time was running out. I had no intention of having a confrontation today. Who knows how I would react if I saw Bergeron. I would be fighting the urge to deck him in the face for what he did to Hailey. Or blast his goddamn balls off.

"Well…" Pablo had to think about it for a moment. "She is no longer… ours." he said. He shook his head as he struggled to bottle his emotions in. "Friends for all these years… just for her to turn on us like this…"

"We need to hold her somewhere…" I suggested. "And get Hailey to safety."

"Guys…"

Both of us turned around to see Hailey sitting up on the couch, though looking fairly weak. *God, am I glad to see her awake*! Seeing her awake was a huge relief to me.

Pablo turned to me. "We can expect that our adversaries will be here very soon…" he said. "And they will probably come for Shannon. We cannot help that. From this moment on, she is an *adversary*. So for now, let's put her in the bathroom and then unplug the refrigerator and push it in front of the door. That way she can't escape on her own."

"So… just keep her prisoner?" I asked. Made me wonder what good that would do since she was going to be escaping anyway. It may have been so that she was not escaping alone. It made sense that she would be more of a threat solo. Not to mention that the handprint reader was going to be offline with the system shutdown. The location was no longer secure. "Abandon base?"

Pablo shrugged. "We have no other choice!" he exclaimed. "They are going to find her here anyway. So might as well leave her in there while we make our escape. (Turns to Hailey) How are you feeling?"

Hailey looked at both of us in a half awakened state, still sitting up on the couch. "Awful headache…" she said. "Looks like… shit hit the fan, didn't it…"

Pablo nodded his head. "Yeah… we can discuss it later."

He pointed at me and then pointed at Shannon. We both picked her up and moved her in front of the bathroom door. Pablo set his end of Shannon down and proceeded to open the door. We laid her down in the bathtub and proceeded to close the door behind us.

"Need anything from the fridge?" I asked.

Pablo shook his head no. "We don't have time, Shane…" he said in a rushed voice. "Whatever we lose we can replace. We have to move this and get out of here."

He moved the fridge out just enough to unplug it from the wall and we both proceeded to push it until it was in front of the bathroom door. While we were moving, Hailey had slowly made her way toward us.

"Can someone ride my bike home for me?" Hailey asked. She looked directly at me.

"Yes, of course…" I said with a smile. *Anything for her right now.* She probably didn't have the strength to ride the distance. Even though

I took no part in this incident, I still felt somewhat responsible for the outcome.

"Let's go." Pablo said, leading us out the door.

While I rode Hailey's bike home, Pablo drove with her as his passenger and she clued him in on her side of the story. Evidently Shannon was already drunk when Hailey arrived. It didn't take that long for the both of them to get into an argument. Hailey had spotted the same case of blackout syringes that I found and confronted Shannon about it. This led to an all-out confession from Shannon about her "deal with the devil" as Hailey called it. While Shannon was still vulnerable from losing friends like Jace and Karl at the protest rally, she was careless and happened to get caught by Bergeron while out and about. Instead of admitting defeat and going to prison, she struck a deal that she would finish the job of the 2042 mole in exchange for her freedom, establishing her role as a "double agent". It turned out she was responsible for the deaths of both George and Randy, having both of them walk into traps. Shamaya was *not* her doing, however. She did not intend on playing her hand so quickly, but Hailey's growing presence at HQ made it difficult for her to conceal her true intentions. Knowing this, the signal given to her in New York by Mitch was the order to proceed, meaning she could reveal her true allegiance if the scenario left her no other choice. In this case, Hailey managed to overpower Shannon when she tried to use the blackout syringe on her and Shannon ended up the one being injected with the syringe, making it impossible for her to cover her tracks. Before Shannon could black out, she hit Hailey over the head with an empty liquor bottle. It was likely after that Shannon locked her devices before passing out.

When we got home, Mr. McFarlane messaged us individually and had us all meet in Pablo's basement for a meeting to discuss what had happened. Hailey had her wound tended to at Pablo's during the meeting. My mom, Gary, and Veronica were all shocked at what happened, although not entirely surprised given Shannon's recent erratic behavior. It was decided that for the time being, it would be appropriate to officially "abandon base" and suspend all AURORA operations until further notice. However, given the new threat Shannon posed being in bed with the enemy, we chose Pablo's basement as the temporary meeting spot. What was ironic was that Shannon's picture still showed on the slideshow for the "enemy of the state" billboards, even though she was already in the hands of law enforcement. Anyone looking for her would be on a wild goose chase.

All of us had particular tasks assigned to us. My mom was to remain undercover with minimal involvement, as Pablo's involvement in the group had increased with Shannon's departure. Maria kept an eye on the Bergerons and remained a wealth of knowledge on that family. Gary and Veronica would continue with their college and be on standby, but also report anything odd from the perspective of the outside looking in. Hailey would deliver messages from her parents about what Troy Bigelow was up to at the police station. It was found that Troy and Muhammad struck up a friendship and were trying to devise ways of bringing the regime down from the inside, but so far they hadn't played their cards yet.

Mr. McFarlane contemplated recovering his equipment from HQ, but decided against it given that the level of encryption was so advanced over nearly three decades of work that even if Bergeron were to try to take it, the equipment was already sabotaged. Not to mention that whatever information was on the servers and computers was probably vaulted by the deep state anyway and they had access to the same exact information. Our database was simply a bootleg of part of the actual internet situated in Utah. The kill switch did its job, and outside of Bergeron's team recovering Shannon, there was no other known activity at HQ. Our base was abandoned, but until they were eliminated, it still wasn’t safe for us to host our activities there. I would spend my time meeting with everyone individually, but often would help Hailey do landscaping work with her parents. I grew to like the job with her. We were taking things day by day because there was no way we were prepared to go on any kind of offensive unless they were to strike first. The ball was now in their court.

# CHAPTER 5

# Mad Science

*November 2045 (at Mitch's Warehouse)*

The Cantrells had a country style home outside of town that had open fields on every side of the property. A lone dirt road could be seen going past it from east to west, with a short driveway spanning about 13 meters from the house. The actual location of the house could be seen from The Ledge at the state park, if one poked their head around where the trees stopped and looked extremely far to the right. There was an old red barn about 50 meters northeast of the house that looked to be abandoned, but underground was a sort of bunker containing a lab. This lab resembled what could be considered HQ for enemy arms. Dubbed "Mitch's Warehouse", Shannon was now setting up her own base of operations here. She played a supporting role for the group, helping them to plan their next moves.

At first there was some animosity because Rico was not happy with how Shannon killed his uncle, but when she explained that Gerald was asked by Adriana to order the hit, he passed the responsibility on to her, which was a secondary meaning of the coded message from Mitch in New York. Adriana wanted ownership of Lucas's strip club, and once she had that she had cut all contact with everyone. She had used the group for her own means and ended up taking the blame for Lucas's death.

Shannon found herself working on a side project with Mitch to make a torture machine. Given Shannon's obsession with sex, it ended up being twisted into a "dopamine emitter." This allowed them to remotely control the human body's pleasure center, more specifically sexual impulses, beyond natural parameters, much like when one "purifies" hard drugs. Shannon had Mitch test the machine on herself, after which she found herself in demand by members of the *League* for her "services". This "service" wasn't exclusive to just the male members either, as even Lynn partook in it.

Used in the Cantrell family since the mid-1970s, this "Warehouse" had been passed down from generation to generation, with Mitch claiming ownership during the last two years. He was especially gifted in the field of chemistry, and while there had been other manufacturers of the infamous "blackout syringe", Mitch had produced his own that had the effect of wiping the short term memory of those that the syringe was used on. These were the syringes that Shannon had at HQ that she had been using on people that were about to figure her out.

On this day, he had Trent and those from the League assisting him in the lab. Mitch brought in a suitcase of materials given to him by his father, and it wasn't uncommon for him to mix a myriad of cocktails for use in his syringes. With Mitch recently becoming acquainted with the *League*, Gerald granted him permission to allow Trent and the others into the lab to take a look around. The shelter was laid out much like AURORA's HQ, except that the hallway with the servers was a second large room about the size of the first room. What was the kitchen area remained so, but shelves upon shelves were kept like a pantry, and while there was a lounge area in this one as well, through the door was the lab. Mitch and Chip just walked in while the others sat around in the lounge area for a moment.

"So what's that case for?" Chip asked, following Mitch to a workbench as he set the case down and began popping the locks open on it.

"All raw materials." Mitch said, quickly opening the case and lining up various groups of substances and chemicals in marked places on the bench. "My father's backroom deals in the medical industry."

"Couldn't you get into trouble for this?" Chip asked. He seemed unsure of himself in such a peculiar new environment.

Mitch paused and turned around to look at Chip, who was now watching over his shoulder. He had a face that suggested 'you have got to be kidding me'. "Since when were you concerned about getting into trouble?" he asked sarcastically. "I might have to start schooling you in your own League. That was a silly question! Anarchy prevails, does it not?"

Chip laughed under his breath, prepared to retract his statement. "Dude, forget I said anything."

Mitch turned back around and got to work. "Imagine the choke hold Trent and Rico would have you under for asking that." he muttered, still facing away from Chip.

"Probably a hard one." Chip said.

Mitch reached over to grab a wireless keyboard that he was using for his desktop machine, which was against the wall to his right. He began typing into a special search engine he had access to in order to do some research on creating a new substance. This search engine was an evolved form of what used to be known as "Tor" and the "Dark Web".

"So, are you creating some kind of drug?" Chip asked curiously.

"I *could* call it a drug." Mitch explained. "One that could possibly have long term side effects. Thing is, I never made a long term one before. I knew I had the stuff to do it, but I never had much of a reason to act on it. That was until Shannon joined us. She is *intimately* aware of our quarry, in more ways than one."

"Hmm… should we use it on Shane?" Chip asked, pondering in thought.

Mitch shook his head no. "I want Shane to see everything come crashing down." he said. "He looks like the type that would buckle the most from stress and fear. So I am not targeting him right now. I need someone more brave… more liable to be reckless. And most importantly, someone that is super close to him. To break his spirit."

Chip grinned and nodded his head. "I think I understand." he said.

"I bet you do." Mitch said, as he proceeded to sort some of the substances on his workbench. "Once I come up with something, we can go somewhere that they frequent. Inject them and take off. But we have to wait for them to be isolated so that they just spontaneously wind up *missing*. If we can't get close enough to inject them, I could also use darts."

As Mitch finished his sentence, Trent walked into the room. He stopped a few steps in and took a quick look around. "So this is your famous arsenal?" he asked, pointing at the workbench he was sitting at.

Mitch looked around in a theatric sort of way, and then looked back up at Trent. "What you see is what you got."

Trent nodded. "I see you're finally ready to get started." he commented.

"All research is done." Mitch said. "I intend on creating a formula with some… *interesting* side effects."

Trent nodded his head and smirked. "I may have my dad contact some... er... *vendors*, from... um... let's just say, *out of state*, in the event that you need it." He said.

"I'll let you know, Trent." Mitch said, turning back toward his work. "I'll get these started for now."

Trent nodded his head, gave a thumbs up, and turned around to proceed out of the room.

"Funny that I'm the only one who can see that you're just *tolerating* them" Chip commented, trying not to laugh. He was enjoying being able to take a step beyond "grunt" status into a possible second in command.

"Of course!" Mitch responded firmly but quietly. "Like I said before, I ain't nobody's bitch. We're all getting along right now, but I am here with you guys on a mission. And hijacking our backsliding government is numero dos on that list. I will let *them* deal with that shit. Not to say I won't get into it later, but my primary goal and Shannon's goal seem to align at the moment. It may be for different reasons, but the ends are all the same."

Chip looked over at the door as if he was anticipating someone entering the room, but nobody came. He turned back to Mitch. "So basically eliminate her old *friends*."

"One by one." Mitch said. He picked two of the chemicals from his case and set them off to the side. "Whatever the case, when this plan is implemented, I want to drag this out… with as much pain and agony as possible. (He puts his finger out) I want there to be *suffering* and the gnashing of teeth. (Puts his hand down). I am going to construct a literal Hell for all of them. That Shane guy seems like an easy victim… he makes it too plain how vulnerable he is."

"Now if only Trent and Rico were on board with that idea." Chip said, taking a step back. "They are bound to want the quick finish."

"They'd better be on board." Mitch said, sure of himself. He turned back toward Chip. "Patience, young padawan. Instant gratification will spoil the fun. Look at this from the point of Tantric sex. Let it build up for a very long time and the climax is going to be explosive."

Chip laughed. "I thought that shit wasn't real." he said.

"For you, it ain't." Mitch said tauntingly, laughing at him and turning back toward the workbench.

"I gotta admit though." Chip said, nodding his head. "I like how you think."

Mitch let out a 'pppssshhh'. "Please." he said, briefly turning back to Chip once more. "What do *you* know about that shit? I was surprised you lasted how long you said you did with those three chicks at the bar. I actually *asked* them because I didn't believe you, but your story checked out."

"Well, I had a lot to drink." Chip said confidently. "Besides, I've got no reason to lie."

"Whiskey dick to the rescue…" Mitch muttered. Then out of nowhere, he began laughing uncontrollably.

Chip raised an eyebrow. "What?" he asked. He was eagerly waiting for the punch line.

Mitch rubbed a tear from his eye. "It sounds like a comic book hero or some shit…" he said. "Whiskey Dick to the rescue!" he shouted, raising his fist into the air.

Chip laughed and shook his head. "He probably works with Dr. Evil on his member shaped space ship."

Mitch nodded his head and grinned. "Still don't know how believable you would be sober, though." He said. "I've got a nice little library on my laptop. If you take it into the bathroom with you, I bet you couldn't last for more than 45 seconds."

"I'll take your word for it." Chip said. He knew what he was getting at and did his best to evade the offer. "I won't give you the satisfaction of seeing me in that light."

Rico walked into the room with a grin on his face. "Aww man!!" he started, turning and pointing at Mitch with both hands. "Mad scientist over here with his plans and shit."

“I’m only getting started.” Mitch said with a condescending grin. “You have to be clever to get around what my family has done for decades in the medical industry. I remember something you said, Chip. About how I was gold?”

“Yeah?” Chip was hoping for some kind of compliment at his efforts to try to be important in the League.

“Well, I’m fucking platinum.” Mitch said. He was boosting his own ego. “And I don’t give a damn who you are, I’ll make that shit radioactive like plutonium.”

“Hmm...” Chip thought about something. “They have Uranium, Neptunium, and Plutonium. Why the heck were they naming these elements after planets? Did they like, run out of names or something?”

“Who gives a shit.” Rico cooed, throwing his arms up. “All we care about is what it does.”

“All I know is that our target had better not make it too easy for me.” Mitch said. He turned to Rico. “I’ll be out there to brief you guys in a second.”

Rico did a mock salute. “YES SIR!” He shouted obnoxiously. He did an about face and went back into the lounge area.

“So, I was actually at the Farmer’s Market the other day…” Chip started. “There’s something that I thought you should know.”

Mitch turned his head and nodded in attention at Chip.

“Shannon is still showing as an enemy of the state.” he said “Even though we have her.”

Mitch laughed. “It’s a diversion, son.” he said, continuing to sort items on his workbench. “And that is why she remains out of sight here. But we provide for her… *needs*… a hell of a lot better than her old friends did. She loves it here.”

Chip grinned and nodded his head. “I can’t imagine why.”

“And who knows…” Mitch continued. He paused and then raised an eyebrow at Chip. “Have you had the chance to… *indulge*… in her services?”

Chip looked down with a timid smile. “Um… not yet…”

“Well, what are you waiting for?” Mitch asked enthusiastically. “Don’t you want the ride of your life?”

Chip chuckled. “Well, yeah!” He said. “Where’s she at?”

“I didn’t mean right this second, you dolt!” Mitch said. He started laughing. “Get on the list and wait your turn like the rest of us.”

He pointed at a datapad in the far corner. Even with his glasses, Chip could not read what was on the screen from the distance. “So she has a sign in sheet?”

“More like an appointment schedule…” Mitch continued. “Now, are you going to be of assistance or should I put you out there with your *friends*?”

“On second thought…” Chip started. The remaining words left him as he made his decision to remain in the lab. He managed to retain his good rapport with Mitch up to this point, and did not want to lose his newfound status.

# CHAPTER 6

# The Achilles Heel

*December, 2045*

Most of the remaining members of AURORA remained in contact with one another, but had diverted off into pursuing their own personal projects. It was as if life was returning to some form of "normalcy". Mr. McFarlane, having burned out on the motivational speaking gig, decided to return home and spend much of his time volunteering and doing community service, although at times he would find that he was useful in other cities and towns across the region as well. He was a common sight at Commerce Square, and though he remained in touch with all of us, he more or less handed the reins for AURORA to Pablo. "I am getting too old for this…" he said. "And I feel like I would be of more use helping out our local community." Thus far there wasn't any resistance from law enforcement against us, but we did our best to remain vigilant. Pablo and Maria were in the offseason for baseball and were focusing on academics, but our group activities as a whole remained suspended for the time being. Unless Bergeron or somebody just randomly showed face, we didn't have much of a mission. It was apparent that Shannon and Bergeron alike had no standing interest in raiding HQ. Pablo and I stopped by there after Thanksgiving to find it was just as we had left it months earlier, save for the out of place refrigerator. My guess was that since Shannon did play her part in building the current version of that system, she probably wasn't keen on destroying her own work.

Gary and Veronica had stopped in town to visit us last month, but both were studying for final exams soon after. They have kept a low profile but both of them seem to be taking care of each other quite well. It was like old times meeting in Pablo's basement. Hailey and Veronica played a game of pool just for fun and of course Veronica won, but Hailey had it down to the wire. It was an impressive display to say the least. Hailey and I ended up playing next to make up for the game we didn't get to play at last year's party. She started out in the lead but ended up knocking the 8 ball in prematurely, securing my victory. "You actually beat me at something for once." she said. *A win is a win.*

What was funny is that all of us were feeling pretty chill that night and Pablo actually convinced those of us who had never smoked pot before to join him and Maria in a circle in his living room. I thought Hailey was going to crash, but she toughed it out. We all had a fun time telling funny stories and laughing about things in our past. Hailey told a story about being at a beach in North Carolina five years ago and they were doing a JAWS re-enactment. She wouldn't stop yelling "Shark" and would pick the funniest moments to yell. I told a story about going with my dad to his work at the Auto Shop in early 2039. He had a rusty Chevrolet truck on the hoist and he accidentally set off the alarm. It had a total of eight horns turned to different notes and it began playing an old southern Bluegrass song from the 1800s called "Oh Suzanna." It almost sounded like it was being played on an accordion. He and three other mechanics, laughing their asses off, sang what words they knew and clapped their hands to the rhythm of the song, some of them making up their own words to the song. Pablo was at Catholic Mass with his parents in the fall of 2035 and the priest's robe caught fire. Veronica told a story about how she and Shamaya were waiting for their parents to pick them up from a church event four years ago and they were waiting by the main highway, which was busier than normal. They were urging passing cars to honk their horns and this huge semi-truck drove by and had a horn so loud that it knocked them both off their feet. Maria couldn't think of anything at the time and when we got to Gary, he was like "Yo… I'm blitzed." and we all laughed. That was a fun night!

In general, I spent most of my time either hanging out with Hailey or helping my mom around the house, or both. Since winter was approaching, the Burnett's family business slowed down. My mom had suggested that during the off season that they try their hand at having a small greenhouse in Commerce Square where they could sell various small indoor plants. This was a unique market and it didn't appear that many others were doing it. Of course, this had helped them enough to pay the bills, but it was still far less than what they got during the summer with their landscaping business.

-------

Hailey spent much of the day keeping her parents company at their stand in Commerce Square. With the holidays in full force, the demand for potted plants like ferns and such had noticeably increased. She walked into the Farmer's Market pushing a two decker cart containing six potted fern plants, three on the top and three on the bottom. She had to find Bernice so that the ferns could be properly labeled and stocked. Cutting through one of the center aisles to get to the back, she ended up finding Bernice in the freezer section.

"Hailey!" Bernice looked up from her cart. She was labeling and stocking items in the freezers. "How've you been, dear?"

Hailey rolled her cart past Bernice and parked it on her opposite side so that they both would not block the aisle. "My parents are selling plants on the side during the off season…" she said, pointing at the ferns. "These are ready to be put up for sale."

Bernice looked at both decks of Hailey's cart. "I see…" she said. She turned back to her work but continued talking. "I am almost done with these. Maybe you can come with me while I drop this empty cart off and I will help you find a place for those."

A woman who looked to be in her late 20s strolled into their aisle from the front end. She was about 176 centimeters tall with a mid-sized frame, and had dark brown hair that went down just past her shoulders. The black and gold sundress that she wore was reminiscent of a hippie or bohemian style trend. Her nose had piercings on both the septum and right nostril, and she had tribal tattoos on both of her arms. Hailey did not recognize her, but Bernice's jaw dropped and she opened her arms for a hug. The woman smiled and embraced her, but she seemed like she was in a state of urgency.

"Helen, you've returned!" Bernice said, as both of them let go and looked at each other. "How's life over there in Arizona?" she asked.

"Doing alright, I guess…" Helen said, looking down and then looking at Hailey. "I'm sorry if I was interrupting anything here…"

"Oh no, you're fine…" Hailey insisted. She studied Helen's demeanor for a moment. "You seem like you're in a hurry."

"Unfortunately, yes…" Helen said. She turned to Bernice. "To answer your question, Kaiden and our daughter are doing just fine. But the real reason I am here is to figure out what is going on with my sister."

Hailey's face went a ghostly white. Helen noticed her reaction. "You mean Shannon?" Hailey asked, noticing the resemblance.

Helen nodded her head. "You know her?" she asked. She had a serious look on her face.

Hailey nodded her head. "Truthfully, I wish I didn't." she said. She made an attempt to conceal her uneasy vibes, but it seemed that Helen was able to pick up on them.

Helen smiled with a look of reassurance. "Can't say that I blame you…" she said. She turned back to Bernice. "I saw a billboard with her listed as an enemy of the state… in Sedona… half of the country away. Which I am not surprised but something is fishy. I saw on the news that they are only supposed to be within a 100 km radius of their last sighting. I know for a fact she's *not* in Arizona."

"I haven't seen her in years…" Bernice said, pointing at Hailey. "But Hailey here and her friend Shane both were acquainted with her up until recently."

Helen turned to Hailey. "My condolences…" she said sarcastically.

"She told us a sob story of how her family abandoned her…" Hailey said. She paused to ponder. "But I am guessing she didn't tell the whole story."

Helen laughed. "Of course she didn't!" she said. She seemed to have not been surprised by this. "Shannon is the spitting image of our narcissist mother. Well… maybe a lesser version, but both are just as bad. I am married with a family now and I did not want to subject my daughter to that kind of dysfunction. But unfortunately our parents followed me to the same town and we couldn't afford to move again. Our great uncle Viktor paid for my trip out here because even *he* believes that something is going on… and that says a lot given that he was born in the Soviet Union."

"Where is Shane now?" Bernice asked.

"Probably at home…" Hailey said. She turned to Helen. "I wish I had time to take you to him, but both Bernice and I are kind of on the clock right now. I can call him to have him meet you here at Commerce Square."

"That'd be great…" Helen said. She looked over toward the exit and then back to Hailey. "Thank you. (Turns to Bernice) I'm sorry that I didn't have time for the formalities… but if we all figure out what in the blue hell is going on, maybe afterwards we can catch up?"

"That'd be wonderful!" Bernice said. She put on her usually cheesy smile. "I won't keep you then! Hailey, you know what to do! I will get this cart back to your parents when I'm done."

Hailey nodded her head and walked out the door with Helen, leaving her cart in Bernice's care. She typed a message on her WCD to Shane.

*AT YOUR EARLIEST CONVENIENCE, SOMEONE IS WAITING FOR YOU OUTSIDE OF FARMER'S MARKET. SHANNON'S SISTER. SEEMS URGENT. -H.*

"That's a nifty little device…" Helen said, noticing Hailey finishing her message. They stopped outside of the Farmer's Market and waited.

"You won't have to go far…" Hailey said. She was avoiding the topic of the WCD for the time being. Having just met her, she had no intention of volunteering information. "I told him to meet you here." she turned to Helen with a smile. "It's safer that way."

Helen smiled. "I appreciate it." she said. She reached out to shake Hailey's hand. "Your name was Hailey, right?"

Hailey nodded, taking the handshake. "Yes…" she said. "And I think you have already made a better first impression than your sister."

Helen scoffed. "That's not hard to do…" she said. Both of them stood outside of the news stands in front of the building. "I suppose that until Shane arrives, formalities do have a *little* bit of time, right?"

"Maybe…" Hailey said. She was noticeably fidgety. "Although I can't stay long. Duty calls."

"Oh, don't let me hold you up!" Helen said. She had a slight smile. "It's not like I am a stranger to this town or anything. It's just been a while."

Hailey nodded and prepared to be on her way. "I'll catch you guys later!"

They waved goodbye and Hailey made her way down the strip. She was a little bit apprehensive that Helen was Shannon's sister and was looking for a reason to escape. She continued walking. Her parents were working clear at the other end of Commerce Square. Beyond the Square were the municipal buildings and then the actual downtown, which included the jail at the opposite end. Winchester had a weird layout about it.

Hailey walked along the northern edge of the square before the cement gave way to grass. From the edge of the grass, the forest that led to HQ was a stone's throw. As she was walking, she found herself distracted by the sights of nature. There was no snow on the ground but it was a somewhat comfortable 6 degrees Celsius. The grass in the forest, what parts of it weren't covered by leaves, remained a pale green, and the leaves ranged from red to yellow to orange. The trees were particularly easy to see through with how bare they were. The sun was shining overhead, and if not for the wind being calm, Hailey may have needed more than her aquamarine colored windbreaker. As she observed, a beautiful eastern bluebird flew into the forest but perched on a low branch just inside. Hailey proceeded to follow it. The bird chirped and flew to another tree several meters further into the forest. She stopped a meter from the tree and looked up. The branch that the bird was perched on was only about a meter above her. As she was taking in the sight, she felt a sudden sting in her left heel. The pain quickly became so excruciating that she dropped to her knees, then sat on the ground. Her eyes watered as she winced, with the expression that she wanted to scream, but only a squeaky whimper came out. She slowly took her left foot and noticed a dart of sorts was sticking out of her heel. It was sharp enough that it tore through the fabric on the back of her shoe with ease. She slowly pulled the dart out and took her shoe off, grabbing her foot and rocking back and forth from the pain.

"It hurts, doesn't it?"

Already in a state of panic, Hailey turned and looked up. Shannon stepped out from behind another tree a few more meters back and began to approach her. Hailey began quivering as tears ran down her face, looking at Shannon with a face of defeat.

"I misjudged the drop of these darts…" Shannon said softly, taking the small dart shooter that was in her hand and placing it in her coat pocket. "But ironic where it landed. Nature always was your *Achilles Heel.* That bird? I knew you would chase it. You had said once that you always thought of the bluebird as being *one of the most beautiful creatures with wings*. But with its wings, I have clipped *yours*. Too bad the butterflies aren't out this time of year."

Shannon did a sudden jump at the bird with a hissing sound and scared the bird away.

"Why?" Hailey choked out. Her face was the expression of agony. The thought crossed her mind as well about how cruel Shannon was for scaring the bird away like she did, but she had bigger problems now.

"Oh, I told you why…" Shannon said, folding her arms and leaning back against the tree. "If I eliminate you, Shane, Veronica, Gary. Hell… maybe even Pablo and Maria for good measure, I am a free woman. Does *Operation Bluebird* sound familiar to you?"

Hailey paused to compile a response. What left her lips was shaky but prepared. "A notorious nightmare of human rights violations by the army in India in 1987?"

Shannon sneered. "The name *Bluebird* was also used in the exploration of torture techniques by the CIA in the 1950s, also known as MK Ultra and Artichoke. But that's beside the point."

Hailey was struggling to remain focused but continued to fight whatever was in the dart. "Ironic choice for the name…" she muttered.

"You ain't seen nothing yet!"

Mitch came up from behind Hailey and put her in a headlock with his left arm. She reached up and tried to grab his arms to pull free, but was not strong enough. He put his hand over her mouth and pointed a gun at her head. "You scream. You die. Got it?"

"Why not just shoot me and get it over with?" Hailey muffled, managing to make her speech through the obstruction.

"Now what's the fun in that?" Mitch asked sarcastically.

"And poor, poor Shane…" Shannon taunted, shaking her head slowly. "What's he going to do when he finds out that you are missing?"

"Or even dead?" Mitch continued, looking up at Shannon.

"No…" Shannon said with a sinister grin. "Our device… we built it *especially* for her!"

"That's right…" Mitch said, tightening his grip on Hailey as he looked back down at her. He intended to make the dart work faster at making her pass out. "Wouldn't wanna miss out on all the fun now would we?"

Already weakened from the dart, Hailey fell unconscious. This was the same type of dart used on Shannon when she killed her cell mate in prison and attempted to escape. Mitch got a hold of this technology through Trent, who in turn got it from his father.

"Let's put her in the trunk of your car…" Shannon suggested. She reached down and helped Mitch carry Hailey through the eastern side of the forest until they reached a neighborhood where they parked his black Chrysler 300. He popped the trunk and they set her inside.

"Any last stops before we go back to the workshop?" Mitch asked, closing the trunk.

Shannon gave Mitch a seductive look and bit her lip. "Not if you don't mind me scratching an itch real quick."

Mitch caught on to what she was saying right away. "We may not have privacy." he pointed out with a grin.

"There's an hourly rate hotel in route." Shannon said, turning around and heading toward the front passenger door. She smiled at him. "Check us in, and let me in the back door so they don't catch me at the front desk."

They head to an inn on the way, with Mitch checking them in so that Shannon isn't turned in by anyone watching the cameras for enemies of the state. He opened a side door to get Shannon through. They ignored the fact that Hailey was in the trunk.

*[Queue song: Stegosaurus Rex - Nowhere to Run]*

As Mitch walked into their hotel room, Shannon walked in behind him and shut and locked the door. Both of them sized one another up.

"Well… let's go then!" Mitch teased, rubbing his hands together. Shannon walked toward him and he found himself slowly backing up. He was stopped by the bed. Shannon proceeded to shove Mitch onto the bed on his back and proceeded to get in front of him.

"I don't take orders…" Shannon said, jumping on top of Mitch. "I *give* them!"

Mitch smiled confidently. "Two can play at that game…" he said. In a sudden move he managed to flip her around on the bed to where he was on top. Both of them still had their clothes on.

Shannon smirked in satisfaction. "I'm impressed!" she said. She then grabbed the collar of his shirt and pulled him toward her. "Did you *want* to provoke the animal in me?"

Mitch laughed and grabbed her arms. "I saw all that and more when you tested the machine." he said. "Let me hear you roar!"

Their power struggle would shift back and forth, but they would be evenly matched. Once they tore each other's clothes off, however, it would be Shannon that would end up with the upper hand, as she specialized in knowing how to wear a man down. They would spend the next 25 minutes playing rough before they would finally finish the drive back to the warehouse.

## CHAPTER 7

# The Microchip

My mom dropped me off in front of the Farmer's Market and made her way back to her work. I looked around for anyone who, in any fashion, resembled Shannon. Just up ahead on my right I spotted a dark haired woman in her late 20s who appeared to be looking for someone as well. Her skin tone and hair color resembled Shannon's, and she was a little bit taller and was a medium build. *That's got to be her*, I thought. I stopped in front of her and she seemed to concentrate her gaze at me.

"Hey, are you Shannon's sister?" I asked. She was pretty in her own right. You could tell that she and Shannon were related, but definitely not twins. Not to mention that the sundress she was wearing looked nice on her.

"Yeah…" Helen started, standing up to shake hands. She was maybe 17 centimeters taller than me. "You must be Shane."

I reached my hand out in reciprocation. "Yes. Nice to meet you." I said, as I shook her hand.

A smile formed on Helen's face. "Nice to meet you too." She said, standing next to me as we both faced away from the Farmer's Market. She lightly touched my back and started slowly walking forward.

Assuming that this was a gesture for me to walk with her, I followed her by her side.

"So what brings you in town?" I asked. I was still trying to take this all in. Shannon mentioned that she had a sister but she broke contact with her family long before I met her. I wished my dad were around to counsel me in these strange days. "Why did you need to see me specifically?"

Helen looked down as she talked. "Well, I saw my sister's image on a billboard trying to showcase all the enemies of the state… (looks back over at me) in Arizona."

"It's spread all the way over there?" I asked. Why in Arizona? It was a snowball's chance in Hell that she would even make it halfway across the country.

"Yeah." Helen continued. Her hands were moving as she talked. "What I don't like is how she is some kind of exception to the *100 km* rule… like, what's making her so special?"

"Are you concerned about her?" I asked. My hope was to learn her intent before I proceeded any further with her, just to be safe. The last thing that we would need is for Shannon to have an ally… although Helen probably would have been here much sooner if that were even a possibility.

"For her? No…" She started, folding her arms in front of her and looking down. We both stopped walking. "Why she's singled out? Yes. Something is up with her relationship to the system if they are treating her differently than the other enemies of the state."

"I just might have your answer." I said. I looked over to her and we made eye contact. This must be why she was directed to me. "She had been part of our underground group for a few years now, but from what I was told by Hailey, she secretly made a deal with our corrupt local law enforcement that, if she were to eliminate *us*, she would have her freedom. My guess is they are protecting her, and keeping her picture up as a distraction."

Helen nodded her head. "That makes sense." she said. She and I both looked forward, facing away from the Farmer's Market and watching the afternoon foot traffic come and go. "For what it's worth, I am here to help you guys stop her. There was a reason that we *abandoned* her, and it goes far deeper than you guys even realize. She is very scheming. Is that Bergeron guy still the police chief?"

I nodded my head yes. "Unfortunately." I muttered.

"That just makes matters worse…" Helen continued. "Between her and my mother, I have learned how to both deal with and avoid these people. I am the mother of a young daughter and don't have time for their bullshit. It's my responsibility that the world I raise them in is better than the one that raised me."

We continued walking slowly down Commerce Square. "I feel that responsibility too…" I muttered. Same goals as me. My father definitely wanted a better world for me than what I have been raised in. I am a long way from having kids myself, but my hope is that I have at least some kind of positive impact before they enter this world. My whole goal for joining AURORA in the first place was not only to finish what my father started… but also to see it through to the end.

Helen gave me an awkward look and faced forward again. "My apologies if this sounds personal… but I'm curious…" she started. "Did Shannon try to… violate you at any point?"

My heart skipped a beat and I looked up at her with a surprised look. *How?* Her reputation probably preceded AURORA for all I knew. Back to her high school days. "Y-yes…" I stammered. "Twice that I can think of. If she did any other time I was not made aware of it."

“Mmhmm…” Helen muttered. “Yeah… she hasn’t changed…” she said. She let out a sigh. “I am sorry that she put you through that. Were you with Hailey?”

“If you mean if Hailey and I were together, yes.” I said. *Is almost everybody I know a victim of sexual assault*? I thought. It was clear that I was *far* from the only one. “You know as well as I do that she didn’t care.”

Helen had a look of anger on her face. She clenched her fist, although there wasn’t anywhere to direct that energy. “It’s bad enough I escaped our parents only to end up kidnapped and in an abusive relationship with my ex… Shannon did the same shit to my husband before he and I got married…” she said. There was a quiver in her voice from bottled fury. “Like five years ago. She thinks she can just have anybody she wants, whenever she wants them… or that she’s God’s gift to men…”

“Jeez…” I stopped us from walking and looked at her. “Him too? I am so sorry…” It was validating to know that I wasn’t the only one who was coerced into her schemes. But I felt bad for Hailey and what she had to endure when it was all happening. The thought crossed my mind to mention my dad by name and to see if she found him familiar. Shannon was still living with her family when my dad was still alive. She didn’t even get restricted to HQ until two years after his death because of the medical convention. I suddenly felt sick to my stomach. “When this is all said and done… would you be able to tell Hailey what you just told me?” I asked. “Coming from another woman… it may mean more to her.”

Helen smiled and nodded. “Of course…” she said. “In fact, knowing what I know now, I would be doing us all a disservice if I didn’t. That act of Shannon’s *did* play its part in making me move. Getting out of town was the only way to escape it because she was not going to stop.”

We continued walking. “If I am not getting too personal… how did you two handle it as a couple?” I asked. *I need to be open to anything that can heal these wounds*.

Helen looked forward as she spoke. “Having grown up with Shannon… I know how she is.” she said. “Kaiden felt absolutely awful like he betrayed me. Probably how you felt. But… I felt like I had no choice but to forgive him because, like I said… I know how Shannon is. I know how persuasive and cunning she is. He hated himself for a while but after a while of reassurance, things returned back to normal. But it was the best decision we made to move. No contact was the *only* option.”

This must be why Mr. McFarlane took the risk with his “perfect storm” scenario. He wanted to get Shannon out of the picture as soon as possible because it was only going to get worse for all of us. I was about to respond when, up ahead near the first row of trees in the forest was what looked like someone unconscious lying on their back. The question regarding my father would have to wait. “Hold on…” I said, picking up my walking speed and veering to the right toward the forest. Helen followed me close behind.

“Who is that?” She asked.

As we approached, it looked to be a bristly old man wearing a light blue jacket. He was dressed like he was working in an office building of some kind. I analyzed the face… but then it hit me. “OH SHIT!” I quickly blurted out. *If this is who I think it is, then this is the calm before the storm*. I reached down and checked for a pulse. There was nothing to feel.

“What’s wrong?” Helen asked. She had a trembling in her voice as if she had never seen a dead person before. “Is he… dead?”

I looked up at Helen, nodding my head, and then folded my hands in front of me as I looked down at the ground. I set my WCD to voice-to-text and targeted Mr. McFarlane. "Muhammad Al-Alawi. Dead at 77. Cause of death unknown. Outskirts of Commerce Square."

"Was this one of your... friends?" Helen asked regarding Muhammad.

I nodded my head yes. "Acquaintance." I said. "He had just come out of hiding in February after Shannon and I discovered him in New York. Was off the grid for nearly three decades. He got hired in as a *janitor* at the... police station."

The way I said 'janitor' seemed to tip Helen off on the actual intentions of Muhammad working in that facility. "Maybe he dug for information and got caught." she suggested.

I looked up at her with a half-smile. It was only in 2041 when the rest of the Boyer family jumped ship. Bergeron had long established his foothold around here by then. "Funny that you say that... that is *exactly* why he was there."

My WCD started ringing. It was Mr. McFarlane.

"Shane speaking."

"Shane, where are you? Any idea of how Muhammad ended up so far from the police station?"

"Nope. Helen Boyer and I managed to catch up with one another and we stumbled upon his corpse while out on a stroll." I said. I reached down and felt Muhammad's chest. There was still a faint amount of heat in it, but he was for sure dead. "He has just a trace amount of heat left in his body. He couldn't have been laying here long."

"Search his body. He either wandered out on purpose or was placed there intentionally. Any signs of foul play? Also be careful that it isn't a trap!"

"Not that I can see." I stated. I went to check his pockets when Helen bent down to assist in searching. "And this is in the clear blue open. I don't see anything else to worry about here."

"Hold on, Shane." Helen said. "I found something."

She lifted Muhammad's collar on his right side and noticed a computer chip embedded underneath it. "I thought it was a spider or something at first." she commented, carefully removing the chip and handing it to me.

"Let me know if you find anything." Mr. McFarlane requested.

"We did." I cut in. "He had a microchip pinned to his collar. A clue, maybe?"

"Umm… keep it on your person for now." Mr. McFarlane stated. "We could probably go to HQ and analyze it. But we have another problem. Your mom messaged me and said that Hailey's parents told her that she never returned from the Farmer's Market. I was wondering if you saw her."

My heart sank. "I… I just got a message from her earlier this afternoon…" I started. *Is Hailey missing*? It was taking all of my energy to not go into full on panic mode. I knew how Veronica felt in the school yard when she was in suspense on our search for Shamaya. "The last thing I heard from her was to meet Shannon's sister here. She is here to help us put a stop to whatever it is that Shannon is doing."

"I watched her leave the Farmer's Market…" Helen commented. She made sure that she was near my WCD when she was speaking so that Mr. McFarlane could hear her. "It didn't occur to me to think of escorting her."

"Under normal circumstances, that wouldn't have been necessary…" Mr. McFarlane continued. "But with Shannon working with the enemy now, it is not safe for *any* of us to go anywhere alone. I even told Pablo that he should take Maria with him. Shane, I will have you escort Helen for the time being. Did you bring your handgun?"

I reached down and felt my left side. I had forgotten that I was packing heat, but it was there. "That is affirmative…" I said. For the time being, I was fighting off the pit in my stomach that was worried sick about Hailey's whereabouts, at least until after the call ended. I took the microchip out that Muhammad was carrying and analyzed it. "So, I do not believe any equipment at HQ can read this chip. It is too old of technology. I may need to stop by my house. My dad's old wrist device had a slot for one of these and I can connect it to one of his old laptops."

At about this time, Helen began receiving a phone call on her cell phone. She walked off to the side to answer the call.

"He may have used the old technology to do all of this under the radar…" Mr. McFarlane pointed out.

"Not to mention that it was the technology from his day…" I continued.

"Whatever it is, I want you to concentrate on that first…" Mr. McFarlane said. "You and Helen should see if you can find out what is on that chip. I will contact Pablo about seeing if we can figure out where Hailey is. If we find it necessary to require your assistance, I will inform you and let you guys know of the reassignments as necessary."

Helen got off her phone and made sure she was within earshot of my WCD. "So my Uncle Viktor decided to make his way out here…" she said. "If Shane has to go off and do his own thing, I have another escort lined up."

"Understood…" Mr. McFarlane said. "I appreciate the help, Helen. Although I know that for you this is probably stirring some uneasy memories."

"To say the least…" Helen said. He was probably her teacher as well when she went to high school. "I am going to follow Shane to his house and have my uncle pick me up there. He is getting a hotel room where we can stay during our off time."

"That works…" Mr. McFarlane said. "Be safe you guys. I will be back in town as soon as I can. I will have Pablo and Maria take care of

Muhammad's body. You can be certain that the law enforcement will just leave it there to decay. That's not how I would've wanted him to go."

The call on my WCD ended. I turned to Helen. "We may have to walk…" I said. My nerves were getting the best of me. I trusted that Pablo would be able to handle things, but I had the suspicion that I would end up involved in the search sooner or later, so it was just as well that Helen's uncle Viktor was on his way here. My mind was preoccupied wondering about Hailey's well-being.

"After sitting on that plane for most of the day, I could use the exercise." Helen said, smiling. We headed south and found our way to the street leading to my house.

# CHAPTER 8

# Torture

"So, you captured her by releasing a damn bird?" Rico asked. He was trying not to laugh, but still ended up slapping his knee in humor. "That's pathetic!"

"Shh…" Mitch toned Rico down and had him and Trent huddled near him. He kept to almost a whisper, mostly because Hailey had not woken up yet. "Actually it was Shannon's idea. Operation Bluebird and all. And it worked like a fucking charm."

"My dad told me that she was rather… *tight*." Trent said, looking over at Hailey and then back at the others. "Not that I asked… but easy to understand why the girl was a virgin. She seems boring as shit."

"Not necessarily…" Mitch continued. He cleared his throat, preparing to school them. "They say you should *watch out for the quiet ones*. For all we know, she could have taken all that time she spends by herself to think of things that most of us haven't even thought of. Of course, maybe we can figure that out from her today. But wouldn't it be funny if she ended up being too much for this Shane guy."

"I doubt it…" Rico said, shrugging his shoulders. "If they weren't interested in each other, they wouldn't still be together."

Trent laughed. "They haven't even consummated yet!" he said, looking at Mitch.

"How do you know?" Rico asked. He looked to be challenging Trent's assumption.

"Look at her!" Trent continued, pointing at Hailey, who was still unconscious and mounted on their machine. She had been stripped naked by Mitch and Shannon before being secured. "She looks fresh. If not for my dad she'd *still* be a virgin."

"And if not for me, Shane would still be."

Shannon walked into the room. She looked each of them in the eye before continuing. "I assure you that neither of them have gone all the way yet. Why, I will never understand. But this is here and this is now. I want to see how she responds to all the settings on our nifty little device. Perhaps maybe… *ruin* her for Shane."

At that moment, they could hear a light groaning sound coming from Hailey. She was coming to. Mitch and the others remained quiet and turned to face her, observing her as she woke up.

"Speak of the devil…" Mitch muttered. The four of them looked in her direction.

"Where am I?"

Hailey gazed around what appeared to be an underground bunker. The room was rather dark and appeared to be the same size as HQ, having a similar design, except the floor plan was inverted. The room was a chemistry lab of some sorts, with other high tech equipment along the walls. This was when Hailey realized that she was bound by chains in both her arms and legs, sensors connected to various areas of her body, including her head. She was hanging in a star position vertically from the chain mounts and was also missing her clothes. *I'm naked as a jaybird*, she thought. In front of her, waiting for her to wake up, was Trent, Rico, Shannon, and Mitch. *Great, what do they want*, she thought. As much as she felt violated for being placed on display like this, she knew that crying, complaining or protesting would avail her not. She used up her fear gauge earlier and was all out of fucks to give. Her mind raced to think of ways that she could make herself undesirable to them, if that was even possible. She already was feeling literal hate for all four of them, which was an emotion powerful enough to her that it would absolutely destroy her libido. *That's it*, she thought. This was how she was going to manipulate the energy in her own body to make it physically incapable of "putting out" for them. Her weapon of choice came down to one word: *Defiance.*

"Nice of you to wake up, Hailey." Mitch muttered, folding his arms in front of him and smirking. He was particularly dramatic with his presentation. "I promised these two gentlemen that they could have their way with you as soon as you were awake, and that this lady could watch. And here we are!"

Hailey shook her head in disgust. "I'm revolted." She said.

Mitch laughed slowly as Trent and Rico grinned on either side of him. Shannon folded her arms in front of her and gave Hailey a devious smirk.

"See, Hailey… I think I may fabricate for you a new weakness." Mitch taunted, beginning to pace around in front of her. "With this single switch right here, I will introduce you to a new world of pure pleasure that you… obviously… have never encountered before."

In his right hand, Mitch held a four-button controller that was wired to a machine that was against the wall, which in turn was connected to the chains holding Hailey. He proceeded to slowly tick the up arrow. As Mitch began to push the button on his controller, Hailey felt a warm tingling sensation between her legs, and her chest began to burn. Her heart rate proceeded to increase, and the intensifying feelings were quickly becoming overwhelming. "What…

are you doing?" Hailey managed to squeak out in between pulses. She immediately began to tense herself up to lessen the impact. *I will put up a fight*, she thought.

"Your body is under my control." Mitch declared authoritatively. He continued to flaunt the switch around in front of Hailey. "This switch is directly connected to the pleasure center of your brain, as well as what triggers the feelings for your… sensitive areas. You *cannot* resist it. You can't stop us from having our way with you."

Hailey groaned through the struggle. She smirked. "I won't give you the satisfaction!" she said confidently. "It is *my* body! And you are *daft* if you think I've never pleasured myself before. This is nothing new."

Mitch cut Hailey off abruptly with an impulsive adjustment to the intensity level of his device. A feeling of warmth spread from her pelvic area to the rest of her body. It threatened to consume her like a flame, but she was holding it at bay so far. "I… refuse…"

Shannon looked over at Mitch. "How?" she asked, with a confused and desperate look. "How is she doing this? She should be close to having convulsions by now! Increase the dopamine level, Mitch."

Mitch proceeded to adjust the settings to try to overwhelm Hailey, who seemed to be in heavy concentration to ward off the effects of the machine. "You will wear yourself out!" he said. "And then what? What will you do when we have all but sapped the fight out of you?"

"I do not consent…" Hailey said. Her breathing was labored but she was able to speak through the impulses. "If I want badly enough to *not* give you what you want… then… I have the power… to… not allow you… to take it."

"You have incredible willpower…" Shannon commented, taking a step forward in Hailey's direction. "But it will avail you not if we have to sedate you like Officer Bergeron did."

"Then what's your point?" Hailey asked passive aggressively. "I know you! You want me to have memory of the incident like you forced onto Shane!"

Shannon smiled. "Of course, honey…" she said. "It was too bad your man's will was far too weak for him to even overcome me."

Hailey smirked back. If she weren't bound, she would have had the urge to charge at Shannon and utterly destroy her. She wasn't turned on or aroused at all. She was angry. "It sounds like we are at a stalemate then, Shannon!" she shouted. "You are trying to get me to *willingly* succumb. It's not going to happen! If I am not in the mood, *nobody* is getting any from me. If I do not consent, I don't want it! It's that simple!"

Mitch stepped forward and laughed. "By chance are you the dominant one in your relationship with Shane?"

Hailey gave Mitch her *Pisces Eyes*. "That's none of your fucking business!"

"I'll take that as a yes…" Mitch continued, looking down at his controller. He was analyzing it as if he was trying to figure out another combination to try, but he did not modify the present setting as of yet.

"Shane's a fucking pussy…" Rico muttered. "He needs to know how to be a *man*."

"Shane's a lost cause…" Shannon commented. She looked over at Hailey. "I hope you enjoy being with a *boy* for the rest of your life, sweetheart. A real man takes control."

Hailey shook her head in disagreement. "That's where you're wrong…" she said. "A real man isn't afraid to tell his partner how he *really* feels. Intimacy and truth go hand in hand. Love without authenticity is cowardice."

Shannon laughed. "What about the whole thing with the ballgame?" she asked. "You amuse me. If that was the case, *you* had to teach Shane how to be a man!"

"AT LEAST HE WAS WILLING TO LEARN!" Hailey snapped. "We both made mistakes when we were put under new pressure. I shut him out for something that he had nothing to do with. *That* was my fault too! We *both* had to learn how to deal with our emotions. And he lost his father when he was 12 so who else was supposed to teach him?"

"Oh boo hoo..." Shannon said sarcastically. "I knew Shane's dad for six months before his passing. Heck, I even had my way with him once."

Hailey's jaw dropped in shock. "You lie!" she called out. *The plot thickens*, she thought.

Shannon put her hand over her mouth and did a fake, dramatic gasp. Then she smirked. "Oh? You didn't know?" she asked. "Of course I had to drug him because *he* wouldn't obey me either. I *hate* it when guys like to play the *brat*. Either way, t'was a shame that someone killed him before I could have him a second time. But with or without him, Shane would still have been Shane... and with his mom's history... between you and his father, there must be something about all you Pisces settling for less..."

Hailey lunged forward in fury. "Maybe that is because we see things in people that makes the lot of you *fucking blind*! For better *and* for worse! I *hated* you the moment I sensed your presence the first day Shane and I went to HQ. Guess who was right about their intuition? *Me!* I merely *tolerated* you for the group. You used us! I saw the end before it even began."

"That goes both ways, honey..." Shannon said, twirling a strand of her hair on the right side of her face. "Y'all had some contingency plan for me. Tell me, was I that obvious?"

"You bet your *ass*!" Hailey sneered.

Mitch let out an obnoxiously loud yawn. "I'm bored..." he said, handling the controller again. He set his device to go into maximum intensity. Hailey began screaming and convulsing, the chains making clicking sounds with her every movement. Upon watching her, Trent and Rico each took a step forward. They positioned themselves just short of being on either side of Mitch, as if to keep him in the forefront. Shannon remained behind them, a grin spread on her face.

"Can I go first?" Rico asked, nudging Mitch. He grinned as his eyes bounced back and forth between him and Hailey.

"I… don't think so…" Hailey managed to growl through the intensity of the machine's effects.

"You gonna need lots of lube for me, bee-atch!" Rico teased, taking another step forward to line up by Mitch's side. He began to unzip his fly. "Your eyes gonna go into the back of your head like that…"

"Wait, Rico." Mitch put his hand out to stop him, and turned down the intensity of his device back to the original level again. "We need to see how she handles anticipation of getting plowed."

Trent stepped forward, lining up with Mitch on the side opposite of Rico. "How do you feel, *sweetheart*?" he asked, folding his arms in front of him and pivoting his foot in her direction. He grinned sarcastically as he was anticipating Hailey's answer.

"Fuck you!" Hailey snapped, lunging forward but again being restrained by the chains. It was a relief to her that Mitch put the machine's intensity back to its original levels. She found it far easier to adapt to.

"Feisty still, are we?" Mitch asked, looking back down to his device controller. He began to go through other options on it. "Let's say instead of the all at once approach, I take it nice and slow. Your heart won't be the only part of your body with a pulse."

As he triggered the new setting, Hailey began feeling the effects immediately. A warm sensation traveled with the consistency of steam throughout her entire body. Her breath even felt hotter than normal.

Her eyes squinted shut as she tensed herself to dampen the effect of the machine. But out of nowhere, she began to laugh hysterically. “You guys are relentless, aren’t you!” she called out. She was smiling from the laughter as she spoke. “I admit… I am just as entertained by the fact that I seem to have the power to fuck with you all! You *reek* of desperation!”

Hailey continued laughing hysterically as Shannon remained where she stood, observing with a dumbfounded look on her face. “This is impossible…” Shannon muttered. She turned to Mitch, who had the look about him that he was running out of ideas.

“You know I would rather die than give myself up to you…” Hailey said tauntingly.

“Except we aren’t into necrophilia, Hailey…” Mitch snapped, cutting her off. “Personally, I like my subjects alive… and awake to witness the whole fucking thing.”

Hailey responded with a passive aggressive smirk. “And I like my subjects to take *no* for an answer and respect my decision.”

“Mitch, this isn’t getting anywhere…” Shannon started. She was beginning to see the futility of their efforts to force Hailey into submission, but Mitch did not want to give up.

“NO!” Mitch turned around and snapped at Shannon. He pointed at her with an angry finger. “That *bitch* will NOT show me up!”

Mitch turned back around toward Hailey and proceeded to slap her across the face. “Don’t fuck with me!”

Hailey started laughing again. “Your device made it so I don’t feel the pain…” she said confidently. The machine had the unintended side effect of also releasing chemicals that affected the pain receptors as well. “I’d like to think I have defeated you and your *master plan*, Mitch.”

Mitch looked over at Shannon and then back over to Hailey. “I don’t know how you are doing this…” he said. “But you have made me furious!”

Hailey smiled. "Good!" she said. "I don't give a damn about *any* of you! Truth be told, I am enjoying the fact that you guys can't bend me to your will. I could actually *get off* on that power… but that'll be a pleasure that I will reserve for *myself.* Shane will have a taste one day, but for now we *mutually agreed* to take things slow."

Mitch hastily put all of the controls on full blast, desperate for the desired reaction from Hailey. "I thought I would have worn her down by now…" he said.

Hailey smiled. "It's a lot like how you could keep a vibrator in the same spot too long and it becomes momentarily numb." she said. "I have successfully adapted to your device. *I win.*"

"AARRGGHH!!!" Mitch shouted in frustration and chucked the device's controller on the ground, but miraculously it remained in one piece.

"That's enough, Mitch!" Shannon shouted, making a beeline toward him. She stood in his face.

"What's up with you?" He asked. He seemed rushed and desperate.

"Look at her…" Shannon said, making a gesture in Hailey's direction. "It is clear that we underestimated her. Every effort we make to weaken her is *making her stronger*. Can't you see that? We will have to think of something else. If you keep this up, there will be *no* getting through to her. *STOP!* For now…"

Mitch looked at Shannon with the face of a man who was nursing a bruised ego. He went over to the corner where the remote control for the machine was and retrieved it. Immediately he deactivated the device and turned toward Trent and Rico. "Knock her out. Dress her. Put her in the holding cell."

"Hailey 1, Badass wannabes, 0."

"I didn't give you permission to speak!" Shannon snapped, turning and pointing at Hailey. "This isn't over! Maybe I should try to drag Shane into this."

“Are you so eager for round 2, Shannon?” Hailey asked. Her passive aggressive tone was at full blast. What was supposed to have been a traumatic experience for her ended up being turned on its head with her humiliating her captors. It only made her more confident in herself. “You guys should build a boxing ring in here. You and me. Mono e mono. Let’s go!”

In a swift move, Shannon quick drew her dart shooter from her jacket and nailed Hailey in the right shoulder.

“Well…” Hailey said with a weak smile. “Guess I’ll see you all tomorrow.” She then passed out, her full weight bearing on the chains she was bound by. The dart worked in a matter of seconds thanks to how much of her energy was spent fighting the machine.

“You could have just had me use a syringe…” Mitch muttered, shrugging his shoulders.

“You weren’t fast enough…” Shannon said, a serious tone about her. “And I had enough of her running her mouth. She has a breaking point. We’ve both seen it. But we can’t control her through sexual means. Her mind is… disciplined. Extremely disciplined.”

“I could have my group steak out Shane and Hailey’s neighborhood.” Trent suggested. “Keep Shane on his toes in the meantime. We know where he lives, after all.”

Shannon and Mitch looked at each other and nodded their heads. “Sounds good.” Shannon said. “But first let’s take care of *her*. Get her out of my sight!”

----At the state park---

Maria found herself looking over the horizon from The Ledge. She sat on the ground barely a meter from the cliff, looking down at the field below. The breeze was chilly but not enough to deter her from enjoying the scenery. Pablo had awakened her desire to enjoy the smaller things in life.

(Screeching sound of burning rubber)

The distant sound broke Maria out of the trance that she seemed to be having with nature. She leaned forward and looked to the right, just around the line of trees. Far off into the distance was a house and a barn. But she knew the sound of that car anywhere. It was confirmed by a moving red dot traveling westward on the long valley road.

"What in the world?" she muttered.

# CHAPTER 9

# Nightmare

*December 2045 (days later)*

It has been days and we still haven't received any leads on Hailey. The silence of our adversaries hasn't helped matters much, either. Hailey's WCD was coming back as no response, possibly indicating that wherever she was, it was dead, and our equipment could not track her whereabouts if it lacked power. I had a massive pit in my stomach. *She could be anywhere.* I could point fingers, but what good would that do? Where do we even start? Maria had indicated that there was no traffic in Trent and Rico's neighborhood so they may be out of town somewhere. Gary, Veronica, and Mr. McFarlane were back at HQ restarting all of the computers and working to remove all of Shannon's profiles from the system. Turned out that over time, Shannon had rerouted all administrator access to her account only. Using the same app that had the kill switch, Mr. McFarlane was able to reassign all of the administrator access to himself and delete Shannon's accounts entirely. He was then able to redistribute that access between us, with Pablo receiving most of the emergency access and Hailey and I receiving the standard access. There was absolutely no way that Shannon could get back into the system now even if she did have a sudden interest in our equipment. I was still in possession of Muhammad's chip, which was identified as a MicroSD card. As I suspected earlier, it could be read by connecting my dad's WCD to the computer that Shannon used, but it was also encrypted and we would have to program the system to be able to decrypt it.

Veronica found a second MicroSD card at Randy's desk like the one Muhammad was carrying. Apparently, Randy had made a small pocket underneath the surface of his desk that was hidden from everyone, Shannon in particular. It contained the manuals and how-to's for all of the equipment, including Shannon's trade for building electronic devices, which he gradually threw together while Shannon was, as he put it, "out whoring around". I had only wished that he had told us of this sooner so that we could have dealt with Shannon earlier, but knowing what we know now, he probably had his reasons and was expecting that poor timing of that revelation would not work in our favor. Either way, it was a surprise to see our late associate and friend provide vital information for us in our time of need now.

With nothing to go on in regards to Hailey's whereabouts, Pablo and I found ourselves in his basement trying to come up with ideas. He had pulled the end table from against the wall and positioned it in front of us as we sat on the couch. I needed a safe space to decompress. Last night, the accumulated distress I was feeling resulted in me having a terrible nightmare. I needed to be able to tell someone about it, and I couldn't think of anyone better to do that with than Pablo. If I didn't know any better, also with how he was able to bring Maria around, he would make one hell of a therapist. For someone who was only 22, he was wise beyond his years.

"We have no clues and no leads, man…" Pablo said, looking down at the bowl of marijuana that he was packing for us to pass back and forth. I rarely smoked, but Pablo and I did on occasion. This was something my father wasn't too keen on, but my mom was far more open minded about it.

All of us were worried about Hailey. Her parents have been remaining calm but you could tell that they were holding in a lot of anxiety. My mom was reaching out to them in support and even Troy Bigelow, who was also putting those under his command secretly on alert for any clues leading to her. We had a blank slate of evidence, and this had to change.

"It just kills me…" I started, shaking my head in frustration. I was looking down and then proceeded to look up at Pablo. "Who knows who has her… where she is… what they are doing to her…"

"Assuming that she's even alive." Pablo muttered. He finished packing the bowl and looked over to me.

"Please don't say that, Pablo." I snapped. *She can't be dead*, I thought. It depressed me to think of her not being alive. It devastated me to even think about it. I was less concerned about AURORA at this point. Our efforts to take things to the national level may very well have backfired. The local level was where the problem was, and ironically it was Shannon that said the same. Much like President Barr's education bill. If we took care of our town, and everyone else took care of theirs, we could make a difference. But this would have to take care of itself later.

"Take a couple hits and we'll talk." Pablo turned to me sympathetically, raising both his bowl and his lighter to me with his left hand. "I'm sorry… we just have to place all possibilities on the table, even the worst case scenarios. On that note, we're doing deuces today. I'll give you the honor."

I took both objects and proceeded to light. I took the hit and proceeded to gather my thoughts. "I woke up last night to this dream… even remembering how it started is tricky." I took my second hit and gave the bowl to Pablo.

"Take your time, man…" he said, lighting up and taking his first hit. "This ain't easy for any of us." He took his second hit and handed me the bowl. "You may have to get a little bit more relaxed or you may stammer over your words."

I nodded my head and proceeded to take my hit. It had been since that day we hung out here and Hailey challenged Veronica to that game of pool that I'd last smoked. "It went something like this…"

We would proceed to finish the bowl part way through the story, but I was able to recite it thoroughly.

--------------

Dazed. Disoriented. That's all that came to mind. I had no clue what had just happened, or where I was, only that I lay alone outside somewhere in the damp, cool dirt. I heard the sounds of the crickets, owls and other night tunes in the barely moon-lit forest. I got up on all fours and gazed around me, seeing nothing but woods in every direction. To my left was a tree that looked identical to the one that Hailey and I would normally tie our bikes to. I quickly glanced over to my right. Where there was supposed to be double doors hidden in the grass was just nothing but the grass itself. I knew where I was… at least I thought I did… but something wasn't right.

"Looking for something?"

A voice echoed in a manner almost as if God was talking to me, but it definitely wasn't God. The voice sounded familiar, but I couldn't quite put my finger on it. The suddenness of it startled me, and I fell backward into a sitting position. I looked all around me like a scared animal. This was very strange and confusing. “Alright, I give up.” I called out in a shaky voice. If someone was trying to scare me, they succeeded. “Where the hell am I? HQ is supposed to be over here.” I pointed briefly at the ground to my right where the missing double doors should have been.

“HQ is gone.” the voice said. I now recognized the voice as Mr. McFarlane’s. I looked around to see where the voice was coming from, but I could not find anything. The voice continued. “This is what happens when you allow yourself to be infatuated with *her*.”

“What are you talking about?” I asked in confusion. Before I had the chance to process another thought, an image of Shamaya appeared two meters in front of me toward the left. Mr. McFarlane’s image phased in slowly to her right.

“My death was in vain, Shane.” Shamaya said in a soft voice. She and Mr. McFarlane remained perfectly still, like a pair of ghosts. “You could’ve chosen to focus on tracking down my killers sooner, but you were too focused on your selfish desires.”

Just as she finished her sentence, Hailey appeared out of thin air to the right of Mr. McFarlane. This was not only weird but I was beyond scared at this point. I felt my stomach turn. “You’re a fucking cheater, Shane!” Hailey shouted, pointing her finger at me angrily. “You offered me *no* support! So now I’m taking you down with me!”

Randy appeared next. They appeared to be forming a line in front of me. He appeared calm, but with a look or sarcasm. He shook his head and spoke softly. “I told you that AURORA wouldn’t make it with you and Shannon together. I could’ve told you that. But nooo, I’m just stingy Randy! You’ve done a fine job, Shane… at being selfish.”

*This can’t be*, I thought, gazing around at the silhouettes in front of me. My mind was racing in disbelief. I was confused because

Shannon and I never got together. Perhaps I did screw Hailey over emotionally in the time period in between the isolation ward incident and the parking garage. Maybe it was guilt from "replacing" Hailey with Shannon at last year's baseball game, or the random incidents where I leaned on Shannon for support when Hailey was pushing me away. Or even that trip to pick up our firearms. But this felt blown out of proportion. Perhaps this was a warning of what *could* have happened had Shannon and I actually ended up together and I had officially given up on Hailey. *In what universe would I do such a thing*? I thought. I felt like these were comments directed at a version of me in an alternate reality that did fully succumb to the lust I was feeling toward Shannon. Seeing everyone talk this way to me was unnerving. I wanted to tune everyone out, but I could not. It felt like a bad dream. That was when it hit me. This *is* a dream. A *nightmare*. The reverb behind their echoing voices was a telltale sign, but I could not get myself to wake up. I knew that the longer I endured this torture, the harder it would be for me to face anyone that I saw here, even in real life, and I knew that it wasn't over. A feeling of shame came over me as everything that was being said began to turn in my head like a knife in my chest. I wanted to scream, but I could not get my vocal chords to cooperate. I was stuck here, with more of the people I knew appearing in front of me and tearing into me.

My father was the next to appear, again to the right of the last person. He folded his arms in front of him with a look of disappointment. *Oh no*, I thought. It would've been the worst feeling ever to feel like I disappointed my old man. He was my main source of motivation for fighting for AURORA's cause. My heart sank as I awaited what he had to say. "Haven't I told you, son…" he started calmly. "The needs of the many outweigh the needs of the few? I *knew* Shannon. She is just as selfish as you are. Maybe that's why you two got along so well. But you distracting her has cost all of us."

*We don't get along*, I thought. *Not anymore, at least.* Veronica appeared next to my father. I swore that if enough people showed up, I would have a circle surrounding me. I felt that this was going to end up being the case. "That was wrong of you to do that to Hailey, Shane. Bergeron was your scapegoat and you used him to get out of your relationship with her to satisfy your lust for Shannon. But for what?"

Gary appeared next to Veronica. "HQ. All of us. Gone. Because you let that pretty girl seduce you."

My mom appeared next to Gary. "I taught you better than that, Shane." she said in the same disappointing manner as my father. "When you make the decision to stay with someone, you stick with them through thick and thin. You don't give up on them when it becomes inconvenient. That's like me giving you up because you're making it more difficult for *me* to live." When she said "me", she pointed at herself in emphasis.

"I think there's been a misunderstanding…" I said. Some of this, I could see how it could have happened had different decisions been made at critical times. Hell, a lot of it *did* cross my conscious mind at one point or another. But was I really capable of such betrayal? *This is just my past guilt manifesting itself*, I thought. *Classic case of worry and overthinking*. Yeah, I did a little bit of fucking up early on. But I had long thought that I was over this. Was it really still dwelling within me? Have I not forgiven myself for my mistakes? Maybe it had something to do with Hailey's disappearance and the worst case scenarios of everything were presenting themselves to me. I felt paralyzed. All I could think about was that, if this was a dream, how would I feel when I wake up? Would anyone believe me? I would have to tell *someone* about it.

What I was facing here made me wonder if I had any friends left. I knew it was just a dream, but the emotional pain I was feeling here felt too real. Just then, all of those present began to collectively approach me at the same pace, closing in on me. I began to feel claustrophobic, even though I was outside. I backed up a step but had hit somebody's leg. I looked up and saw Bernice standing over me, holding a disposable aluminum pie tray with both of her hands. "Here's a pie, Shane." she said, with her signature cheesy smile. *Now is not the time for this*, I thought. Just then, she released the pie out of her hands, and it fell onto my face as I looked up. All of the people that were closing in on me stopped and began pointing fingers at me, roaring in loud laughter.

"Guys, stop!" I begged like I was in middle school getting teased. I tried to wipe the pie off of my face, but the more I tried, the more it seemed like it was never ending. There was just more and more pie, as if my head were a pie in itself. In the midst of the laughter, I heard some words through the noise. "Now *that's* like getting egg in your face". But it came from my right. I looked over with the little bit of visibility that I had. Pablo and Marco stood by and gave each other a high five and, along with his baseball team behind him, began laughing like everyone else. I was speechless. There was no worse feeling than what I felt right now. *Am I in Hell or something,* I asked myself. I never had a real visualization or feeling of what Hell would be like… until now. Everyone I care for, or did care for, all ganging up against me. For the first time in my short life, I genuinely felt like I was better off dead. Maybe it was my admission to *enjoying* my experience with Shannon that triggered this. I was feeling all kinds of self-doubt right now.

All of those present began approaching me from all sides. As the first of them grew close enough to touch me, I was blinded by a sudden and quick flash of light. Once again, I was disoriented, but not for as long. *This isn't possible*, I thought. Going from one place to another like that was physically impossible. I practically teleported. This was not three dimensional reality. *Confirmed. This IS a dream*. I took in my new environment and looked around. I was standing by my locker at school. *School? I graduated last year*. That thought seemed irrelevant. If this was another dimension, then time would have no meaning here. But I was here. I could physically interact with the environment, and even suck in the dry air coming out of the ceiling vents. The halls were vacant and the lights were out, except for some light shining through a few of the windows here and there giving just enough illumination for me to see my way. The view outside showed overcast clouds as if it was about to rain, but it was not raining. If I took any steps, they echoed through the empty halls. *I wonder if my locker combination still works*, I asked myself. I turned toward my locker and began working the combination. It unlocked. *At least that's logical.* I opened my locker door, but it was empty. Not even a cobweb stood in the corner. I proceeded to slam my locker door shut, but was startled by the sight of graffiti scribbled on it that wasn't there before I opened it. I instinctively and quickly took a step back.

"What the fuck?" I muttered to myself. This made no sense. I was definitely still stuck in this dream. The graffiti read as follows:

*SHANNON GIVES GREAT BJs*

*LOVE HER? SHE'S THE SCHOOL WHORE*

*MISS BOYER LOVES THE D*

*LIKE HER MOTHER BEFORE HER*

*YOU HAVE NO CHANCE*

I shook my head and backed up a few more steps before turning away. I had to find a bathroom. Everything that I was experiencing was sending me on sensory overload. It was bad enough feeling everybody go against me. Now, it was being egged on with my dream focusing on Shannon's eventful past, even though I did not personally experience it. I stumbled my way down the hall and found the restrooms to my right. I had to wash my face or something to see if it would wake me up from this nightmare. Out of breath, I opened the door. The lights were on, but they were dim. I went to reach for the faucet on the first sink to my right when I heard noise coming from one of the stalls. The noise had ceased once I had stopped moving, but it was enough for me to investigate. *There has to be someone in here*. I thought. I made my way to the handicapped stall in the far corner, and what I saw shocked me.

"Oh, hi Shane!"

It was Shannon. She was wearing only a dark blue bra and underwear, and she had a shirtless Pablo pinned to the wall. She smiled very provocatively at me, with Pablo looking over at me with a blank stare. "Wanna join?" Shannon asked calmly.

I backed up. "No... " I squeaked out. I could not believe that this was happening. The idea of joining in the proposed threesome made my stomach turn. I knew this wasn't real, but it was hard to un-burn this image from my mind. It was also hard to look away, which made it even worse. Shannon essentially had the allure of a popular porn star.

Shannon proceeded to turn back toward Pablo. "Suit yourself." she said sarcastically, and in what appeared to be an effort to please Pablo. "I only want a real man anyway."

She proceeded to make out with Pablo, aggressively and in a manner where it was obvious that it was going to go further. In an act of desperation to get away, I turned and ran out of the bathroom, still out of breath and my chest pounding. I heard sound coming from another area of the building. Continuing down the hall, I quickly passed the bay window in front of the library and found the boiler room. The door was opened to a crack. I opened it the rest of the way and the light from the hallway illuminated Shannon having sex doggy style with a taller, blonde haired boy. *Jace*. I thought. I recognized him from the day Hailey and I met, as well as from photographs. I kept telling myself that this wasn't real, but I could not get myself to wake up. I was forced to endure this misery. “Shannon, what the hell?” I asked, throwing my arms up. I didn’t know what to do, think or say. I was numb. Seeing Shannon have sex with all of these other guys was revolting me. It made me wonder how she made guys feel who were in legitimate relationships with her. *Pablo*, I thought. He must’ve gone through this! In real life! This would explain why he became such an understanding person now. That poor guy must’ve been absolutely destroyed by her at one point.

“There’s a take a number machine at the front office.” this Shannon said sarcastically, glancing at me but appearing to concentrate on the activity at hand. Jace looked over at me for a moment, not saying a word, as he thrust into her, but ultimately faced in line with her. Shannon tilted her head and lowered her eyes to flash her dilated pupils at me. “But you must be this long to ride. Wait your turn, Shane.” she said, winking at me.

I wasn’t insecure about my features, but I was certain that for the sake of this nightmare of a dream that this was supposed to put into perspective just how many people Shannon had been with, both with and without consent, and that I was better off not taking any chances. All cards were stacked against me. It’d be just my luck to expect what I actually have in real life, but then see a tiny nub if I pull down my pants. Dreams were shitty like that. I couldn’t bear the thought of her laughing at me if I ever actually had that issue. I knew that Shannon had far higher than the average body count, and that included the fact that many of them were multiple times. By now, I was growing to expect that everywhere I looked and everywhere I turned, I was going to see Shannon having sex with somebody. I shut the door and continued to run down the hallway.

I approached the front of the school, completely skipping a hallway to my left that contained the principal’s office and other staff offices.

I went through a corridor and entered what was the main lobby, with a hallway with classrooms on my right, the security office on my left, and up ahead in the hallway was the auditorium, cafeteria, and a few conference rooms and lounges. As I passed the security office, I saw that the doors and windows to the outside on my left were boarded up from the inside, seeming to have the opposite effect as boarding up a building would be to keep people out. This intended to keep people *in* the building as if the outdoors were condemned. I went to continue forward in the hallway when I heard a moaning sound come from my left. In a knee-jerk fashion, I jolted in that direction, only to spot Trent and Shannon in the corner where the wall of the security office met the wall that had the boarded up doors. Trent had a topless Shannon pulled against his shirtless body with his hands on her breasts and was kissing her neck.

"I've fucked the captain of the football team before." Shannon casually remarked as she looked up at Trent behind her. She proceeded to reach her hand up to bend his head toward hers so they could make out with her back to him, her body smoothly and slowly waving like a cobra enticed by a snake charmer.

"I'm more of a man than Shane ever will be." Trent remarked, shooting me a look without changing his position with Shannon. Shannon proceeded to eye me as well. "You're fucking hot." she responded.

"Ugh, I can't take it anymore!" I turned around and shouted. My chest was on fire and all of these images were unwelcome to me. I put my hands to my face trying to cover up my eyes. Feeling dizzy and nauseated, I stumbled my way back in the direction I came and got in front of the security office door. *If I can just find a gun, I can put myself out of my misery*, I thought. Maybe, just maybe, if I killed myself in the dream, I could wake up in real life. If this were real life, this wouldn't stop me from doing the same. This felt like an episode of the Twilight Zone. If I couldn't find a gun, I was going to bang my head on the brick walls until I lost consciousness… or pushed my brain out of the back of my skull. Whichever came first. I proceeded to open the door and click the light on, only to find Shannon on her knees giving Rico a blow job. Both of them paused for a moment to gaze their eyes at me. All of this happened so suddenly that I became even more startled than I was earlier, and I could feel the fire of my rage and agitation overflowing out of the vat in which it was contained. I jumped back into the doorway with my hand over my mouth. The tears were finally starting to come. *I'm never going to get out of this torment, am I?*

"Don't be sad, chump." Rico smirked with a careless and casual smile. He was sitting in the office chair with his legs spread. "It's like they say… *you'll never go back.*"

Shannon backed her head up enough to be able to stare at Rico's parts. She traced her fingers slowly on his shaft. "I like it long, hard… throbbing…" she taunted, still eyeing Rico's manhood. She continued her trace on it. "Just look at this vein. I wonder how that'd feel… inside me."

"Pork is on the menu tonight." Rico smiled, turning his gaze from me back to Shannon.

In a hurry, I took a step back, turned around and slammed the door shut. I booked it in my original direction again, aiming for the end of the hall past the cafeteria. *The parking lot is out there.* I told myself. *Stay calm. If you run and watch your feet, you'll make it.* I wanted to scream, but nothing was coming out. There was a massive pit in my chest that I could not shake for the life of me. I had never felt emotion of this magnitude before, but I wasn't so sure that I could handle it either. The emotion could only be described as desperation. The need to escape. I took off running toward the end of the hall. I felt the breeze against me, but the hallway felt the same distance as when I first began running, as if I were running in place. Still, I kept going, hoping that I was getting closer. I got to the corridor two meters from the entrance to the parking lot before I tripped on the metal floor divider at the first set of double doors. I fell on the ground, but as I was quickly about to get back up, I looked against the wall to my left and saw Shannon with Lynn.

"These tats are hot, Lynn." Shannon said with a smile, tracing her hand up Lynn's tattoo sleeve on her arm. "The punk look is good on you. I'd take you over Shane any day."

Both of them looked right at me the moment Shannon finished her sentence in a manner that was taunting and provocative. Their smiles together looked evil enough to please the devil himself. At that moment, they put their arms around each other, pressed their bodies against one another and made out. *When is this ever going to end*, I thought. I couldn't take any more of this, but it didn't matter where I ran, the torment was everywhere. Part of me actually found this scene to be the easiest one for me to stomach, but the fact that it involved two women that I wanted absolutely nothing to do with ruined it for me. I quickly made it to my feet and stormed my way out the door. When I made it out, I kept running until I rounded the corner on my right. Out of breath, I leaned against the wall, falling down into a sitting position. I was ready to scream. I looked around to see no one outside, no cars on the road nearby, but a few vehicles were in the parking lot. A green Cadillac. A blue Honda. A red convertible. A black Jeep. I recognized the first three as Pablo's, Shannon's and Trent's, respectively. The Jeep must've been Jace's. I looked forward, where the track field was down a hill up ahead. It was cool, breezy, and cloudy out, matching my gloom and melancholy feelings. Just then, my WCD received a message. *My WCD*! I forgot all about it. I reached to check it and it appeared to be from Mr. McFarlane.

*WHY ARE YOU ON CAMPUS? SCHOOL IS CANCELED!*

"I don't know…" I muttered to myself, proceeding to clear the message from my device. "Tell me how I got here and we'll call it even!" How would he even have known that I was here? Was he watching me? Was this some sort of test?

I got up and sprinted toward the parking lot. I looked to my left as I passed the front corner of the school and saw a bike rack there that was never there before… with my bike in it. I changed directions and began heading over to it. I didn't care where I was parked, I just needed to get the hell out of here.

"Confused, Shane?"

I turned around startled and in fear, almost losing my balance as I turned. My heart sunk at the sight. "How did you get me here?" I cried, shaking my head. A massive pit developed in my stomach. "Get out of my head!"

"It's my nature, Shane." Shannon said, moving her hands as she talked like she characteristically did. Her facial expression, however, was emotionally dead. "You know me. I just can't get enough."

I shook my head. "Hailey was right about you." I said, angrily pointing my finger. It was the truth. From now on, if she has a bad vibe about someone, I'm going to fucking listen to her. "I feel like shit for even directing *any* of my attention toward you. You're really slick, you know that?"

"All the time, every day." Shannon said with a smirk, taking a step back as if to pose her body for me.

"No…" I said. That was *not* what I meant by "slick". By this time, Shannon had obstructed the path to my bike. "I've had enough. Let me go."

Shannon proceeded to grab me and pull herself against me. "Welcome to the astral plane, Shane." she said. "You are a little more aware than I would have liked, but I can still control you."

*Son of a bitch.* "You intentionally brought me here?" I asked. "But how?" I have had a couple of conversations with people about this sort of thing in the past, but research on the expanded universe was hard to come by these days. For some reason the world governments saw knowledge of other dimensions and metaphysical phenomena as "dangerous". Even HQ was short on information. At the time Mr. McFarlane built the databases, censorship of that genre of media had already taken place. Word of mouth was the most reliable source of information.

"Come on, Shane." Shannon said, smirking. "You already know the answer to that question."

She reinforced her hold on me. Involuntarily, I had hit arousal instantly upon her touching me. *Holy shit…*, I thought. This *couldn't* be real. I looked into Shannon's eyes as she stared back at me, biting her lip seductively and looking ready to go. Her eyes were either red or extremely bloodshot. Something wasn't right. I blinked and could've sworn that I saw the face of a demon, like something reptilian, but it flashed before my eyes and then was back to Shannon again.

Suddenly, things began to fade to white, and the sound was fading into what sounded like white noise. I could tell that a struggle was starting between Shannon and I in the dream, but it appeared that I was phasing out of that environment. As things faded, I felt myself breaking free. I had woken up. It took several minutes for me to sort through my mind what was real or not. I had to tell someone. Pablo was my best option.

-------------

That nightmare felt so real that my experience with it was nearly indistinguishable from actual memories. I used the idea of discontinuity as a means to separate fact from fiction. I had never had a dream of that nature before, as if it were beyond nature itself. The evidence for that being the case is convincing. My guess was that it was driven by the energy of the psychological torment that many of us have felt as of late. This was a formula that drew from my deepest insecurities and regrets, amplified them, and threw them in my face in the form of a nightmare. From what I was able to gather, the first half of the dream was my own doing. But that left me so vulnerable that, somehow, Shannon was able to take advantage of it. I used to believe that people were crazy when they said that things like this happened to them. This sure as hell made a believer out of me.

"Is there anything that you heard that catches you by surprise, Pablo?" I asked. My stomach hurt thinking about all of the possible responses that he could come back with at this point. It was nice being able to get that off my chest, but it had utterly destroyed me last night.

Pablo looked forward and sighed. "Yes and no." he started. He turned his gaze in my direction. "It was true in the following senses. Shannon… while outwardly may not have been as bad in real life… I wouldn't put it past her to be as much of a freak as she was in your dream. In fact, your *exaggeration* could have been a well-hidden reality. As weird as this sounds, I think you experienced some sort of psychic attack from her. That intensity is unparalleled by anything that we could experience in the normal sense."

"What about that first part?" I asked. "With everyone turning against me?"

"I think you are still being hard on yourself for feeling like you betrayed Hailey." Pablo said. "It may seem that way, but to be honest, Shannon did to *many* others what she did to you. You said that her sister even confirmed this to try to take some of the weight off of your conscience."

I nodded my head. "She did…" I muttered. Helen proverbially led me to water, but couldn't make me drink.

Pablo paused for a moment and then continued with his feedback. "I found it interesting how you were seeing her in different areas of the school engaged in… extracurricular activities like that. When I was with her, that was about how many times I had to endure it before I finally broke it off with her."

"So you actually experienced that?" I asked. *My God, I was right*!

Pablo folded his arms in front of him and nodded. "Not all in one fell swoop, of course…" he said. "And obviously not the exact same people… except for maybe Jace. But over the course of a few months, those happened sporadically. I confronted her in the parking lot one day much like you did. Told her that I had enough."

I nodded my head. "I am… really sorry she put you through that…" I said.

Pablo put his hand on my shoulder and smiled reassuringly. "Don't be." he said. "We've all been there. I'm over it. Seeing Shannon's true nature, I am sure also that Hailey has already forgiven you, and you are *not* her only *victim*, so to speak. You need to forgive yourself!"

I sighed and buried my face in my hands. "The first order of business is to find Hailey…" I said, looking back up. "I…"

Pablo gave me a hug to try to comfort me. I wanted to cry, but I could not get the tears to come out. Everything in me was all stopped up, including my words. I missed Hailey. I wanted her to be ok. But I knew everyone else was concerned about her too. I could only imagine how her parents felt having their only child turn up missing like this.

Pablo put his hand back on my shoulder. "Let's stay positive…" he said. "Manifestation could go a very long way here."

As he finished his sentence, my WCD started going off. It was my mom.

<BEEP><BEEP>

"Hi mom"

"Shane, listen to me. Do *not* go home! Our house has been ransacked."

"Where are you now?" I asked. What the heck would people want with our house? It wasn't like we had anything valuable there.

"Pastor Kevin is letting me stay in the basement of the church for now. I can still get to work and what not, but that is where you will find me for now."

"Who told you?" I asked. "Was someone there?" My emotional energy had been spent reviewing my nightmare. I found myself responding in an uncharacteristically stoic manner.

"Mr. McFarlane stopped by my work. He said that whoever you and Helen found by the forest… I guess he was carrying something that the police wanted and they saw you take it. ...Please tell me you no longer have it?"

She was speaking of the microchip that Muhammad was carrying. Now it was more obvious than ever that there was something critical on that chip that we needed. "I gave that to Mr. McFarlane off site. It's at HQ for safekeeping."

Of course, this was a lie. I had it on my person at this very moment. It was probably a good thing because they would probably ransack HQ next. As I thought of this I had an idea.

"If you do stop by there, do not go alone and make sure you're armed. I have to go, but I needed to make sure you were in the loop. I love you, son."

"Love you too, ma. Stay safe."

The call ended. I looked up at Pablo. "Things just keep getting stranger…" I muttered.

"You… didn't leave it at HQ did you…" Pablo guessed. He was reading my body language as I was talking to my mom, apparently. He knew as well as I did that our adversaries knew where HQ was, and now they would have a reason to go there.

I shook my head no. "I have it on me..." I said. "I know better. My mom don't need to know. I gave my dad's WCD to Mr. McFarlane. What we should do is backup the information on Randy's chip and use that as a decoy while I keep the real thing on me... until we can decode it with every one of us present and we can guard HQ from invasion. We should probably warn Mr. McFarlane."

Pablo nodded. "I agree..." he said. "But in person. I can't trust that our WCDs are as secure as we hope with Shannon now on the opposing side. Good idea keeping the components separated, though."

# CHAPTER 10

# Fortified

A day had passed and Pablo had let me stay the night at his house. He met with Mr. McFarlane and briefed him on a proposal to put HQ back into lockdown mode in the event Shannon or Bergeron make an attempt at an entrance. He proceeded to do so and informed the rest of us that we would meet on a case by case basis, and any critical conversation would be made in person.

I had heard nothing more from my mom about home, although she did text me that if anything came up that she would let me know. I felt well rested and ready for the day. The couch actually wasn't bad to sleep on and I felt like sleeping more, but I had things to take care of. I sat up and reached to the end of the couch to grab my jacket and my gun holster. *Glad I didn't leave that at home*, I told myself. I needed to get to a phone and call Helen's cell. Helen already knew about my WCD from when Mr. McFarlane contacted me the other day. Heck, I'll set it to private and call her on that.

<BEEP><BEEP>

The phone rang on the other end. At the end of the 2nd ring, she answered.

"Hello?"

"Helen, this is Shane. Are we still meeting at Commerce Square?"

"Yup, how soon?"

"30 minutes or so." I said.

"See you then."

Short and sweet. That's all I was hoping for with that call. I rushed up the stairs and Pablo was in his kitchen reading news tabloids on his tablet. "There's donuts on the counter. Help yourself." he said, without missing a beat. He didn't look up from his tablet when he spoke.

I went over and selected a glazed donut out of a half-dozen box. There was also a half-gallon of Orange Juice sitting on the counter. It was still cold. I took a clear plastic disposable cup from a sleeve of them behind the OJ jug and poured some in. "Thank you, Pablo." I turned to him and commented appreciatively. I looked around and had realized that I had not seen Maria for much of the time that I was here. "Is Maria keeping a low profile?" I asked.

"She has been spending *a lot* of time at the park lately." Pablo said. A slight smile cracked on his face, but he was still reading his tablet. "I thought she would be afraid to go out, but she insisted that she had *something to investigate*. Out of nowhere she got this sudden interest in meditation. But it is helping her so I am supportive." He looked up from his tablet at me. "Need to go to Commerce Square?" He asked.

I nodded my head yes. "Helen is going to be waiting for me." I indicated. I took a bite of the donut and then a swig of the orange juice. I was going to take it for the ride.

He got up and we both headed to his car. Commerce Square wasn't far from his house at all, but driving was quicker than walking. At least he was closer than my house was to the meet up point.

When we got there, a burgundy Buick, from the late 2020s, was waiting there with its engine running. It was her uncle Viktor driving, and Helen was the passenger. I exited Pablo's car and approached the

Buick. The Buick shut off and both Helen and her uncle got out of the car. Seeing this, Pablo determined that it was safe to leave and proceeded to exit the parking lot. Helen leaned back against the car as her uncle slowly made his way to our side. I approached him and he reached his hand out to shake mine.

"You must be Shane!" he said. He looked to be in his 70s and stood at about 178 centimeters tall. We briefly shook hands. "I see you're acquainted with my nephew's daughters. I'm their father's uncle Viktor. Viktor Vasilyev."

Vasilyev. The name sounded familiar. I remember Shannon mentioning that name when we took the road trip to pick up our guns. His family must've been the one with all the arms connections to Russia. *I am face to face with someone who was my age when the Soviet Union still existed... and he lived there!* I had to let that sink in for a moment. Talk about the history involved. He seemed to have retained his Russian accent all these years.

"Shane Conliffe" I replied. A feeling of confidence came over me that I normally would not have attributed to times where I met new people. The next question left my lips involuntarily. "You've probably heard of my father, Corey Conliffe."

"Yes…" Viktor said quickly, putting his hand back to his side. "I was interested in his editorials on the Internet. I never had the chance to meet him in person, but we networked online quite a bit in the 2030s. He was a smart man."

I had yet to meet someone who *didn't* have some kind of admiration for my father. At least, outside of those in Bergeron's network. Better yet, not a single person had asked who he was. They all seemed to know the name. Kind of strange, if I say so myself.

"Yeah… I do miss him from time to time." I mentioned. What was sad is that even though he was killed only six years ago, my memories with him were beginning to fade over time. It was a good thing that I surrounded myself with people who actually knew and met him. This meant that he was still with us, and they could help in keeping his memory alive.

"What's the mission today?" Helen asked.

"We need to stop at my house." I said. "I am armed, so we can go and make sure that things are cleared out. Some of the things that my father had stored in various places in the house are irreplaceable and may be needed later to stop Shannon. I have to make sure everything is intact."

Viktor nodded his head. "Well, let's go then." he suggested.

We got into the car and he drove us to my street. He let us out at the end by my mom's work so we could get in through a back way. I was sure that the front of the house would obviously be the least safe. We speed walked down the street.

"Let's pass the house and get in through the back door." I suggested. Helen followed closely behind me as we kept walking. I was careful not to point at the house in case someone was watching. I nodded my head in its direction instead. There didn't seem to be anyone in sight, but that didn't mean that they weren't lurking. Something was telling me to still be careful. "That pale yellow house ahead on the right is mine. 3853."

"Got it…" Helen muttered nervously. We were just now passing the house.

"Sharp right at the fence." I directed. The fence divided our property from that of my next door neighbor, but the backyard was accessible without even jumping a fence. *That's something that'll have to change in the future*, I thought. We made it along the right side of the house and were about to clear the last corner.

"Well, what do we have here?" a female voice exclaimed.

I was startled by the fact that I wasn't expecting anybody to be guarding the back door. Of all people, Lynn was the one stationed there. She stood against the side of the house as if she were anticipating my arrival. She looked over at Helen, seemingly annoyed by the fact that she was with me and didn't get me alone. *You're outnumbered*, I thought.

"What are you doing at *my* house?" I started, putting my hand out as if I were stopping her. This was bizarre. I didn't expect that my house would still be staked out by the time I returned to it. It was as if they had a round the clock rotation to guard it… from me.

"I've been told no one in or out." Lynn said calmly. She looked away and toward the fields behind the fence as she spoke.

"By who?" I asked hastily. *Who is really going to lock me out of my own fucking house?*

"Like I'm gonna tell you." Lynn sneered, rolling her eyes and turning back in our direction.

Helen took a step forward. "We don't have time for this." We were still a few feet from Lynn, but she was a pace ahead of me. "Let us into the damn house." she said authoritatively.

Lynn looked like a shrimp compared to Helen in size, but I had no time to warn her not to underestimate her.

"I have my orders." Lynn said firmly, appearing to calm down for a moment but emanating the stench of having a short fuse. "No one in or out without authorization."

*Oh, what the heck*, I thought. I took a step forward to get next to Helen in support. "Bullshit. I live here."

"Who's authorization?" Helen asked, putting her right hand on her hip but leaving the left one straight down. She appeared to lean her weight on her right side, appearing to get slightly closer to me.

"City government." Lynn said, not budging from her stance.

"Perfect!" Helen exclaimed hastily, shoving Lynn out of the way and barreling past her to get to the back door. It appeared that she had just as much potential to have disregard for the government as her sister once did. Helen was able to get her left hand on the doorknob, but Lynn regained her position and spun her around so that she was facing her. In a sudden move and as if it were rehearsed, Lynn pulled out a knife that was hidden on her side and jammed it into the left side of Helen's chest.

Helen looked like she was about to scream, but what came out was a barely audible gasp. I couldn't believe what I just saw. I felt petrified in fear, just standing completely still where I was as Lynn removed the knife from Helen and replaced it back into her holder. Helen, while holding her bleeding left side, buckled at the knees and fell to the ground, her body beginning to shake as if she were on the verge of shock. Seeing Helen on the ground shaking was enough to send a jolt through my chest and give me a swift kick in the ass to make a move. As I rushed toward Helen, Lynn stepped over her to put herself between me and the back door of my house. Reclaiming my home had become second priority. Upon bending down on my knees in front of Helen to support her, I looked up at Lynn and drew my MP443, pointing it right at her. "Get out of here, Lynn. NOW!" I shouted, fighting off tears. Helen was nothing like her sister. In all she seemed to be a real sweetheart. I suddenly found myself extremely protective of her.

Lynn grinned from ear to ear. She folded her arms in front of her as if to call my bluff. "Very well, Shane. Let the rage build inside of you."

I fired a shot without hesitancy over Lynn's right shoulder, forming a nice round hole in the vinyl siding of my house. She jumped, not expecting me to shoot. The look on her face was priceless, showing a great amount of surprise. "GET THE FUCK OUT!" I screamed.

Lynn quickly took a few steps toward the left corner of the house, a slight smile cracking. She turned back toward me for a brief moment.

"We'll be after your ass, Shane." She said coolly. With that, she disappeared around the corner.

As she left, I looked down at Helen, who seemed to be fighting off the traumatic shock that her body was trying to force itself into. Her hands were still on her left side as she was laying on it, her body lightly shaking and her face wincing in pain. Her breathing sounded like how someone would shiver in the cold. *It is practically winter*, I thought. It was mid-December. I looked down where her side was resting. The now blood-stained dress that she was wearing was not going to protect her from the elements for long.

"I'm calling for help." I reassured, taking my shirt off and putting it to her side in order to help slow the bleeding. I was wearing just my jacket, but that was all I needed. Helen needed to be kept warm. She instinctively allowed me to move her arm enough to where she could hold the shirt in place and remain in her current position. I sat next to her and leaned in order to put my arms around her gently and lightly. I wanted to help minimize her shaking. She was almost in a fetal position at this point. It saddened me to see her like this when I knew that she had a family to go home to. The tears streaming from Helen's eyes felt like they could've been mine. If she died, who would tell her daughter what happened to her mom? How would her husband handle it? All of this went through my mind as I dialed Mr. McFarlane with my WCD.

<BEEP!><BEEP!>

"This is Shane. Helen has been stabbed! I don't know where to take her because we were brought by her Uncle Viktor. I don't have his contact information."

"I just signaled for Pastor Kevin to head your way." Mr. McFarlane stated. "I have a feeling that there will be a lot more of that soon. Bergeron is organizing a turf war."

"What does that mean?" I asked. *Great... that's just what we need. Street warfare.*

"It means that gangs, cops, and what have you, have all teamed up to take over the town by force. It is up to us and those who refuse to follow along to stop them. Pablo is already arranging with Marco on getting their old gangs back together to defend the town against these... mercenaries."

"We are probably going to be heavily outnumbered." I pointed out. "How the hell are we going to manage that?"

"We had an unexpected breakthrough as of earlier this afternoon." Mr. McFarlane stated. "You probably knew this but it is public knowledge now. Troy Bigelow is organizing his own alliance against Bergeron and can use all the help he can get."

"Ohh ok…" I started. I still had yet to meet Troy, although I had heard a lot about him from Hailey and her family. "What's the scoop?"

"He assisted Muhammad in his espionage." Mr. McFarlane continued. "He gave him access to the computers when no one was looking and made available the classified information that Muhammad stole. Troy got questioned about it yesterday and at that point, initiated an insurrection inside of the police station. This whole thing is about to blow wide open, Shane."

I nodded my head, but then it occurred to me he couldn't see what I was seeing through the WCD. "How long before the pastor gets here to help Helen?" I asked.

"He shouldn't be long now." Mr. McFarlane said. "Your mom is in the basement of the church and she is going to be helping with any injured of ours that come along. We were already preparing for this before you even called."

"Ok." I said. "Make it quick, though. I think there is internal bleeding. I took off my shirt to help slow it down, but there might be something vital damaged."

"We'll take care of her." He reassured. "I sent Gary and Veronica to the church as well. I am following right behind as we speak. Our first priority is to help the injured, as the hospital is going to have their beds full. Once we get Helen situated, I have Pablo picking you up again. You two are going to concentrate on finding Hailey. Once she is found, those of us remaining will go to HQ to decode that chip. We will need a numbers presence there to guard it from invasion."

"If I find some leads, I'll let you know." I said. Helen began moving slightly. "I have to tend to Helen until the pastor arrives. Shane out."

As I terminated the call, Helen turned slowly from laying on her side and leaned on me, breathing heavily. She raised her head lightly as if she were trying to tough it out. "I'm… getting dizzy, Shane." she said weakly, her head lowering into a place of rest on my lap.

"Stay with me..." I said calmly. A fire burned in my chest as I let my hand make a single pass across her long, straight brown hair. I was determined to make her comfortable, in hopes of keeping her mind off of the possibility of dying. "Help is on the way." I calmly reassured. "This is not the end." My heart pounded as if I were looking down at the edge of a cliff. I didn't know if that were going to come true or not, but regardless, I had to try. Positive energy often had its benefits at times like this. As Helen rested her head on me, I eagerly waited for the pastor to show up so he could transport us to safety.

<BZZZT!>

*What now?*, I thought. I wasn't off the WCD for 30 seconds when it buzzed yet again. A text message this time. I touched the screen to view it. It was from Maria. *When did she get a WCD*? I guessed that Pablo reprogrammed Shannon's old device and gave it to her.

*"POSSIBLE LEAD! HAILEY COULD BE HELD CAPTIVE UNDERGROUND BY MITCH. LOCATION SEEN FROM THE LEDGE. LOOK SOUTH. WHITE HOUSE. RED BARN."*

Wow. Maria of all people found a lead. I was going to have to notify Pablo at once. This must have been why she had been at the park so much. I definitely underestimated her ability to observe her environment.

# CHAPTER 11

# The Warehouse

When the pastor arrived at my house, we carefully picked Helen up and loaded her into the bed of his red 2040 Chevy truck. He had avoided the street altogether and drove through the grass fields that were behind the fence in my backyard, eventually backing into the fence to break enough of it away to allow us to pass through without going on the other side of the house. I rode with Helen in the bed of the truck to make sure that she remained stable. The church was only a couple minutes away from here, and he seemed to know the smoothest path on the grassy field to reduce the bumps. While on the way, I forwarded Maria's message to Pablo. I had yet to receive a response from him.

We arrived at the church and Gary was waiting out front for us with a stretcher. Pastor Kevin pulled in front of him and shut the truck off, and quickly exited the cab and ran to the back to allow Helen and I to exit the tailgate. Gary ran up to the back of the truck with the stretcher.

"Take the back, Shane" he said, moving to the front. I did as he told me and we put the stretcher horizontal with the truck bed so Pastor Kevin could move Helen onto the stretcher.

"She's on. Go!" He exclaimed. It appeared that he was going to go re-park his truck, probably to leave the path clear for other potential patients.

Up ahead, my mom and Veronica were holding the doors open for us. "Right this way." Veronica said as we passed through the corridor. They led us to the basement through the wide handicap ramp so that we could avoid the stairs. There were no elevators.

When we got down there, I noticed that the entire church basement was set up like a makeshift infirmary. Stretchers lined the walls, and while there were not many occupants here yet, it gave me chills anticipating what they could possibly be preparing for. Mr. McFarlane pointed at an empty spot on the left for Gary and I to set Helen down on.

"We will take care of Helen." My mom reassured. Her voice was rushed almost to the point of panic.

"What's going on, mom?" I asked. My voice was shaking with anxiety. I was still feeling shaken from seeing Helen get stabbed right in front of me, let alone from the fast pace of everything that was going on. I could feel myself approaching my sensory limit.

"It's about to be an all-out street war." Veronica stated, answering for my mom. "Gangs and good cops vs. bad cops and politicians."

I nodded my head. *Like classic cops and robbers*, I thought.

"Did you make it inside the house?" My mom asked, as she bent down to address Helen's wound.

"No…" I said, hanging my head. "We got there and someone was guarding it. Helen tried to barrel through and she got stabbed. I fired a gunshot to scare the person away, and decided that I had to help Helen first. If you see a bullet hole in the siding in the back of the house, that's why."

My mom kept her eyes on Helen's wound, but nodded her head in response. "That's trivial…" she muttered. "We'll take care of that later."

"Do you have any leads on Hailey?" Mr. McFarlane asked.

I nodded my head. "Maria Matheson, of all people." I started. "Found a possible area to investigate. I was trying to treat Helen at the time in the back of the pastor's truck so I couldn't call Pablo, but I sent a text and have received no reply."

"What did it say?" He asked, taking a few steps forward. He was walking slowly enough for me to anticipate that he was expecting me to meet him halfway. I showed him the message from Maria and the one I sent Pablo.

"Call him." Mr. McFarlane instructed. "I want you to scope out that area."

--- ---

"The Ledge?" Pablo asked. "Are you sure about this?"

We took the country road leading up to the old farmhouse that could be seen south of the Ledge, but hadn't reached our destination yet. The forest where the state park was could be seen in the distance to our left. It couldn't be very much further. Pablo had wondered why Maria hadn't told him anything about this lead until the last minute. Evidently she wanted to be sure before reporting it so she continued gathering evidence.

"That's exactly what I was told." I explained. "When Hailey and I were out here last year on our first *date*, if you will, I do remember seeing this house out there. I didn't pay attention in regards to the barn, but the geography fits what I am aware of."

We continued down the street until a white house appeared on the left. There were other houses peppered along the road, but it was the only white house.

"This it?" Pablo asked.

“I guess we’ll find out.” I commented.

Pablo made the car hang a rough left and we found ourselves driving in the grass. Dirt kicked up from the rear tires as it moved. This car was rear wheel drive, a rarity for this time.

“Dude, you can’t even find shocks for this anymore!” I exclaimed. A 1996 Cadillac Fleetwood was hardly a household name now, let alone when my parents were my age. This car was a dinosaur even then. “Be careful!”

“I got my tweaks.” Pablo said coolly. He continued driving and passed the house on its left side, still driving through the field. Up ahead on our left was a red barn. There was another red barn just like it in the distance further back, but I assumed that our target was the one closest to the house. A rusty 2010’s white Ford truck was parked outside of it, albeit poorly. They must’ve had no parking coordination here.

“That’s got to be it, Pablo.” I pointed out. “Park on the opposite side so we can face the street. That way when we need to make an escape, we can just go.”

“Not a bad idea…” Pablo said with a grin. He had pulled around the barn and stopped as I had suggested. “I hope you know that we are not going to know what condition we will find Hailey in when we get in there, right?”

I sighed. “If she’s in there…” I said.

Pablo shifted the car into park and the doors automatically unlocked. He chuckled under his breath. “Wow, did you hear that?” he asked, looking down at his steering wheel. “The automatic lock and unlock hasn’t worked with my shifter in years on this thing, and out of nowhere… click!”

I nodded my head. “The perks of an old car…” I mentioned. I wanted to try to add some light to the situation.

Pablo glared at me and shut his engine off. “Let’s go.” he said firmly.

We got out of the car and he locked the doors before he shut his door. The barn wasn't even that large. I couldn't see how anything of use could be in here. Plus, all the doors were closed. There was a white side door as well as a garage type door in the front. "I think we can assume that these are locked." I said as we approached it.

Pablo pulled out a bobby pin from his pocket and grinned. "Haven't I taught you anything, Shane?" he asked.

I looked back over at the side door. There was a padlock on it. "No…" I muttered. "And honestly that is a lesson I would have expected from Shannon."

He lifted the padlock on the door to where the keyhole was exposed. I stood behind him to observe what he was doing. "Who do you think taught *me*, genius?" He asked sarcastically. Just then the padlock came unlocked. "Here goes nothing." he said, taking the lock out of the rings and opening the door. We both walked inside as Pablo discarded the padlock on the ground.

"Dude…" I started. I couldn't find the words for what I was seeing. Boxes upon boxes of chemicals and controlled substances, all stored in totes and cardboard boxes lining the walls. In the center were a few workbenches, and in the back was a large cabinet that more likely contained medical instruments than tools.

"Freaky shit here, huh?" Pablo turned to me and commented. We were both gazing forward at the cabinet at the back of the barn.

"What are we looking for?" I asked. The more I looked around, the less it looked like that anyone, or anything, was here that would lead us to Hailey.

"Just… keep something in mind." Pablo started. "For all we know, this is a setup. What we are looking for may very well be concealed. (He turns toward me and begins moving his hands as he talks) Consider the remote location out here. You're packing heat, right?"

I lifted my jacket to briefly reveal my holster.

"Good." Pablo continued. He slightly lifted his jacket to show his concealed weapon as well, except it wasn't a stun gun. It was an actual firearm. "Now for a little test."

He tapped his foot on the ground and waited for a moment. He then tapped it again, but even harder. The sound had a slight echo. "Could they be underground?" I asked.

Pablo smiled and gave me a thumbs up. "Look for a storm door," he suggested. "One similar to HQ."

Both of us began to scout the floors. There was obviously no other dimension of this structure besides the floor that could lead anywhere but outside. If there was anything in here, it had to be on the ground. Other than the ground being made of mostly dirt, there wasn't much of any kind of camouflage. That was until I spotted something unusual about the middle workbench in the center of the room. "Pablo, come here." I said.

I waited for him to come up behind me before I wiped away some dirt that was a slightly lighter color than the dirt on the ground in the rest of the barn. I started brushing it aside, uncovering a lock. It was unlocked!

"Quick, open it!" Pablo recommended. "Someone was probably just here."

I looked on all sides of me and then looked up. There was a bucket of dirt directly above us hanging on a pulley. The pulley looked like it led to some kind of machine sitting in the corner. It was probably a mechanism to cover the door up in dirt when someone opens and closes it so that it keeps it concealed. Good idea, but they probably recycled the dirt so often that the impurities took over the color. Without further thought, I removed the lock and opened one of the doors. The doors were much lighter in weight than the ones to our HQ. I was sure that the wood was thin enough for me to just kick my foot through it. I pointed to have Pablo go first.

"Is the coast clear down there?" he asked.

I shrugged my shoulders. "I'm going in after you." I said. I didn't know what we were going to be facing down there. But I was as prepared as I was going to be.

Pablo went down the steps and I followed behind him, closing the door as soon as I had enough room to. It was a small room much like the one in our HQ where our handprint reader was located, except there was no door. We went right through. This layout was also pretty standard, except that their kitchen doubled as some kind of doomsday pantry, and most of the lights were off down here. There was a lounge area in the same exact far corner also, except instead of the computers and equipment, there was a lot of lab test equipment lining the walls on the right. We made it to the end where there was a small hallway that, in our base, would have led to the server rooms, but in this case, it was blocked off with a door requiring a 4 digit code on a numbered keypad. *Great*, I thought.

"Fat chance of figuring out the combination here…" I said quietly.

"Give me a sec…" Pablo whispered. He began fiddling with his WCD.

As I was thinking of an idea of my own, I heard a small squeaking sound. As if by instinct, I turned on a built-in emergency flashlight on my WCD and shined it at the ground. A white lab rat scurried its way past us and into a hole in the wall to the left of the door. I looked back up at Pablo. "There is something behind that door that they don't want us outsiders to see…" I continued quietly.

"Reflect your light on the buttons to see which ones are worn." Pablo suggested.

I nodded my head and turned back toward the keypad. The 1, 2 and 5 keys looked a little more worn than the others and had residue of human skin oil on all three keys.

Pablo drew his WCD within whisper distance and began speaking a command into it. “Codebreaker. Delta. Two. Sigma. Alpha. Psi.” He positioned the WCD directly in front of the keypad and shot a sly grin in my direction. “I’ve always wanted to have a reason to use this…” he muttered.

I nodded my head. This must have been some sort of command that only the “high ranking” members of AURORA had available on their devices.

Pablo began to explain how it worked. “Between the worn keys, the possible combinations with those keys, and the resonating frequency of this keypad, I should have the code scanned soon.”

I was getting nervous the longer that this was taking, but fortunately it was only another few seconds before Pablo’s WCD began a rapid flash to indicate the completion of the code break. He shut the backlight off on his WCD and rapidly typed 1-5-2-5 into the keypad.

A green light lit up and I heard the lock unlatch on the other side. I couldn’t shake the butterflies that I was feeling in anticipation of what I thought I was going to see behind this door. In a spike of bravery, I quickly opened the door and stormed through with my hand on my gun holster. Pablo followed behind.

# CHAPTER 12

# The Moment of Truth

The place was not that well-lit, or most of the lights were not active. From what I could tell that was close to me there were tables and tables of chemistry equipment. Beakers. Tubes. Even syringes. *This is sick*, I thought. The environment here gave me the chills. I was about to continue moving forward when Pablo put his hand on my shoulder to stop me. I looked up. A mini heart attack ensued. "Hailey!"

She was chained, nude, in a star formation in the back of the room to what appeared to be some kind of machine. It looked like something medieval. Before I could approach any further, a single bulb chain light clicked on to Hailey's right. Trent and Shannon made their way out of what appeared to be yet another room behind this one. *Shannon, you bitch*!

Trent looked over at Pablo and I, and then drew his cell phone from his pocket. Looking both of us right in the eye, he began talking into it. "Mitch, we have two unauthorized personnel in your warehouse. Get back here now!"

I stared down Shannon, who had an emotionless face about her. I shook my head in agitation and put my hand out in Trent's direction. "What the hell?"

"She's with us." Trent sneered. "Our *secret weapon*. Thanks to her, we know what shenanigans *all* of you are up to."

Shannon drew a gun and pointed it at Hailey, who looked weak and malnourished. "One more step. I shoot." she said.

Seeing Hailey like this was breaking me. She appeared to be lighter weight than normal. Not to mention that they would just leave her chained up in a vulnerable and unnatural position with no clothes on. "This is… *barbaric*!" I cried out. The sight was horrifying.

Trent pointed his gun at Pablo. "You probably should hold your steps as well." he said. "I don't give a damn that you are a soon to be celebrity. I will move your ass from the sports section to the obituary."

"I told you they'd come…" Hailey muttered, barely moving.

Just hearing her voice was soothing. But this was no time to let my guard down. At least feeling the presence of her consciousness was giving me the strength I needed to endure being in this twisted room.

"Shut up, bitch!" Trent looked back and shouted. "Don't make me turn up the dopamine emitter again."

I was confused. A *dopamine emitter*?

"That's inhumane as fuck, Trent." Pablo stated in a raised voice. His mind was processing at a quicker rate than mine. Whatever two and two is, he put them together. I had a feeling that I would need to lean on Pablo's wisdom to function so long as we remained here.

A slight smile cracked on Hailey's face, but her eyes remained closed. She let out a small chuckle. "Didn't you guys learn your lesson the first time?" she asked.

"We made modifications." Shannon barked, grabbing the controller with her free hand and turning in Hailey's direction. "I can assure you we got it right this time."

Shannon proceeded to dial up the emitter and Shane and Pablo saw for themselves what the machine was supposed to be capable of. Yet once again they ran into the problem of Hailey resisting it.

"So this…" I was at a loss for words. Pablo and I looked at each other in horror and looked back over at Shannon.

Shannon continued my sentence. "...Is supposed to take over the pleasure center of the brain." she said. She locked the hammer back on her gun. "But your girl has been seriously prude. She's no fun. No wonder you don't get any, Shane."

I looked over at Hailey and smirked. "We decided on that mutually…" I said. *You go, girl!* "I can assure you that if she is not interested, there is nothing that will change her mind. By trying to force her, it makes her not want it even more. She will literally block the impulse with her conscious mind. You're empowering her."

"See, he gets it…" Hailey said softly. A proud smirk developed on her face. My heart raced knowing that was for me. *I got your back, darling*!

Shannon turned her gaze toward Hailey, gritting her teeth and her eyes going black. The gun trembled in her right hand and the control module in her left. "Nobody asked you, bitch…" she growled.

"It's a pity that you picked such a weak man, Hailey…" Trent said. "Shane couldn't resist Shannon's advances. He's such a pussy. A real man would have made you have sex by now."

"A real man respects his woman…" Hailey said. "And Shane respects me."

Pablo remained silent as he observed the exchange of banter in the room. His gun was still low key pointed at Trent.

"I guess it was *very* respectful for him to let me have my way with him, huh?" Shannon teased, a devious smirk coming across her face.

"You're an exception to the rule…" Hailey said. "You will force *anybody* to fuck you. Tell Shane what you told me."

Shannon eyed me with an expression of resistance.

"Tell him…" Hailey insisted. "Or I will."

Shannon's eyes went black again. "If you tell him *anything*, I swear…"

Hailey took a quick breath as if she were preparing to harness a hidden reserve of strength. "Shannon fucked your dad!" She blurted out.

I gasped. "Jesus Christ, Shannon!" I raised my gun at her with trembling hands, but I was still fearful of firing my first shot. *She even took advantage of my father?* There was absolutely no limit to this woman. This was going to take a good long while for me to process.

Shannon hauled off and backhanded Hailey in the face with the butt of her gun. "I warned you, bitch!" she screamed. She then turned her gaze toward me. "Now that we're telling each other's secrets, I'm surprised that Pablo hasn't told you yet that he was at the scene of the crime when Corey was murdered!"

My heart did a quick drop in my chest. "WHAT?" In a swift movement I lowered my gun and turned in Pablo's direction. I didn't know how to feel about this, but I was not ready to have this conversation when everyone had their guns pointed at each other. He instinctively sensed my shocked emotion but had his eyes concentrated on Shannon. I looked back over to her just in time to see her pointing her gun at me point blank while I was not looking.

<BOOM!>

"AAAAHH, GOD!!" Shannon let out a shrill scream as she dropped both the gun and the controller to the emitter. She fell to her knees and clutched her right hand in pain, which was clearly dripping blood. I looked over at Pablo again, who was now pointing his gun at Trent. There was smoke coming from the barrel. "I'll explain later Shane…" he said with a serious tone. "But for now, pay attention. She almost had you."

I wanted to be angry that he kept this from me for so long, but at the same time, knowing him, he probably had his reasons. Pablo always had trouble expressing his emotions. Maybe he just didn't know how to tell me. Either way, I am at least willing to give him a chance to speak when the time comes, and he did just save my life.

Trent started to laugh as he alternated his gun's aim between Pablo and I. Shannon remained on the floor, down for the count and clutching her hand. "Ahhh, yes… now I remember…" Trent started. He took a couple of steps to the side as he spoke. "My father ordered that hit."

"Of course he did…" I muttered. I did not know who to direct this to at this point. It was all of a sudden beginning to make sense why everyone knew more about my father than I did.

"Don't worry…" Trent continued. He paced back the other direction, still wavering his gun at both Pablo and I. "Your friend here was NOT the one who pulled the trigger. In fact, you can be assured that he was too chicken shit to even try. A fella in his gang named Billy-Mac was your poor dad's killer. But don't worry, he's long dead himself."

"And I quit the gang right after that." Pablo continued. His expression signified fury. "That sight of him in the car is one that has haunted me for years!"

"Don't forget…" Shannon started. She was speaking softly trying to hold back the pain from her gunshot wound. "You quitting the gang was also influenced by *me* telling you that I knew him. *Two degrees of separation*, remember?"

I looked at Shannon and Pablo glanced at her. He seemed focused on Trent but felt the need to respond. "Yes… you are right about that…" he said. *Give credit where it's due, I guess.*

"I may have violated him, Shane…" Shannon continued. Her vibe reeked of insincere empathy. "But I was *not* in any way responsible for his death."

"And that's supposed to comfort me?" I snapped. "For some people, the trauma of the violation *leads* to their death. Often self-inflicted. You have some fucking nerve…"

"But Corey didn't say a word to you or your mom, did he?" Shannon taunted. "He went back to his jolly good life as if *nothing* ever happened or even bothered him at all! What do you suppose that says about him as a person, hmm?"

"You probably wiped his memory." Pablo said.

"No… I did not tamper with his memory." Shannon sneered. "Knocked him out, had my way, sure. But that's like Shane not remembering having his little altercation outside of the debates last summer. I didn't have that tech in 2039!"

Trent picked up where Shannon left off. "What's the last thing you remember before my dad and I jabbed you that day, huh?"

The more I thought about it, the more uncomfortable I was getting with this conversation. I still remembered everything. Getting punched and then jabbed, and remembering my WCD being in standby as I felt myself fading. But I had no such details of Shannon taking advantage of me in HQ before my birthday. Only vague recollections and memory gaps. But what Shannon was saying had the potential of possibility, and it made my heart sink.

Shannon smiled. "I rest my case…" she said. "What if he kept some secrets? What if he lived a double life that you and your mom never knew about? Why do you think everybody *knows his name*? What if he wasn't the man you thought he was all those years? What if… you have been idolizing a *fraud*?"

"ENOUGH!" I shouted. The fury swelled within me, enough to make me tremble. I made sure my gun was pointing at Shannon. Pablo's was still aimed at Trent. I shook my head in disbelief. "I will not let your gaslighting tarnish the memory of my father!"

Shannon shrugged her shoulders the best she could with the pain that she was in. "It's not like we can actually prove these theories wrong, Shane. What was it he used to quote? Eliminate the impossible, whatever's left, however improbable, must be the truth? Sherlock Holmes or something?"

"Psshh, who cares!" Trent barked. He started pacing again. "*My* father, who is still alive by the way, is taking his rightful place. He is doing his job… ridding the town, and now the country, of pitiful maggots like you guys."

"Looks like we have a standoff, Trent…" Pablo pointed out. "Don't be an elitist prick. You have ten seconds to put down your gun or I will shoot. And I'll shoot to kill this time."

Pablo began to count down and I saw Shannon, who began shaking and was in tears, eyeing her gun. In a sudden movement I moved and kicked it across the room and away from her reach. I wasn't taking any chances, even if her adrenaline was wearing off.

"You bluff!" Trent taunted. He was waving his gun back and forth between Pablo and I. "And to think of who to shoot first…"

Trent pointed his gun at Hailey, but before he could shoot, Pablo pulled the trigger and shot him point blank. "Time's up…" Pablo muttered. Trent fell to the floor dead. "Who's the pussy now?"

Both of us turned toward Shannon, who sat on the ground looking up at us.

"Why… did you spare me?" Shannon turned to Pablo and asked. "Just kill me. I deserve to die."

"That's the coward's way out." Pablo said. "*You* will answer for your crimes."

She softened her eyes, although I knew better than to believe her expression at face value. "You don't still have some kind of feelings for me after all these years, do you Pablo?"

Pablo scoffed. Shannon narrowed her eyes and had a slight smirk on her face.

I was about to speak when a door opened on the opposite wall. I reached for my gun.

"WHAT THE F…"

Quickly and without hesitation, I turned around and fired two shots at whoever it was without looking. Part of me was screaming on the inside *Dude, what the fuck? What if you shoot the wrong person?* Lucky for me that wasn't the case. I had to do a double take for it to register who had fallen to the ground just a couple meters behind me and to the left. It was Rico. *Sorry, not sorry*, I thought. One more adversary down. It suddenly hit me that I had never killed a man before. Until now. If I could venture a guess, that was probably Pablo's first kill too. I had reason to believe the conversation that just took place. Pablo was simply another instance of being in the wrong place at the wrong time, with the wrong people. *That must be why he relates so much to Maria.* I still didn't know how to process Shannon's wild theories about my father.

Pablo pointed his gun at Shannon. "Tell me how to free Hailey from these restraints."

"Psshh…" Shannon scoffed. "You're smart. Figure it out!"

Pablo fired a round over Shannon's head to startle her.

"Alright!" She screamed. "Twist keys. Disconnecting all four will shut down the machine. Then you just have to detach the sensors from her noggin."

Pablo kept Shannon in check. "This feels like Deja Vu…" I commented, proceeding to unlock Hailey. I was prepared to catch her to soften her descent to the floor. "The four of us in the exact same condition the day we abandoned HQ."

One by one I was able to twist them off, starting with the legs so that Hailey could get them used to moving again without being stiff. After I got her arms released, she leaned on me and appeared to be standing on her own somewhat, but still relied on some level of support from me. It was understandable considering that she had been stuck in the same position for at least a while. She managed to find the strength to jettison the sensors herself. I felt my heart flutter as Hailey's bare body was leaning on me. Her skin was cold to the touch from prolonged exposure to the cold basement air in the middle of December. I did a quick scan of the perimeter for her clothes but nothing was within my viewing range.

"You mean…" Hailey began to talk softly, her voice weak. But a smile to indicate that she wanted to keep her sense of humor, "My tired ass… Shannon's decapitated ass… and you two peacemakers?"

Pablo smiled at Hailey, even though she barely had the strength to open her eyes to see it. He pulled a pair of rubber gloves from his pants pocket and proceeded to put them over his hands. "Something like that…" he said. "Except for one thing."

In a sudden movement, Pablo took a blackout syringe from his coat pocket and used it on Shannon before she had time to react. She seemed to give up the fight for now.

"Did you bring that from HQ?" I asked. At this point Hailey decided to sit on the floor next to me.

Pablo nodded his head. "Yep…" he said, discarding the spent syringe by chucking it underneath one of the lab tables. "Right from Shannon's old desk. I kept it for this occasion, and thanks to these gloves, my fingerprints won't be on it."

I turned toward Hailey. "Any idea where they kept your clothes?" I asked.

"There is a holding room on the other side of this machine…" Hailey said calmly. "It's in there."

She didn't seem to be making a big deal that she was naked. As I got up to retrieve her clothes for her, Pablo called Mr. McFarlane.

<BEEP!><BEEP!>

"Any luck, Pablo?" Mr. McFarlane asked.

"We have her." Pablo said. "But she is in rough condition. She will likely need medical attention but she isn't too critical. Maybe some food and some sleep will do her well."

"Excellent..." Mr. McFarlane said. "I will let everyone know that she is ok. Anything else of note?"

"Trent and Rico are dead." Pablo continued. "Self-defense. I have Shannon here with a gunshot wound to her right hand. We decided to spare her so that she can answer for her crimes once the dust settles."

*Maybe we can be the ones to get the reward money*, I thought.

"Alright..." Mr. McFarlane said. "Bring her here, but restrained. You are to remain with her until the appropriate law enforcement is handed custody. Not only that, but she will also answer to her family that is here."

"Copy that..." Pablo said, disconnecting the call.

While he was talking on his WCD, I was concentrating on listening to the conversation and neither of us noticed that Hailey made her way over to Trent and had squatted on him before getting dressed. Pablo and I both looked at her in disbelief, but we were holding back the urge to bust out laughing. *Did she really just piss on him?*

"What?" Hailey asked, pulling her pants up and beginning to put her shoes on. She had sat back down about a half meter from Trent's body. "They were very stingy about bathroom breaks when I was on that machine. And... I thought that it would be payback for the isolation ward." She looked up at us and grinned sarcastically. "I'm all out of fucks to give today. It's not like he has a grave I can piss on or anything. Yet..."

I put my hand over my mouth and chuckled. At any other time I would question this, but I felt that I was better off leaving this one alone. It gave me a little bit of pride on how well she could hold her own and stand up for herself. *That's my girl.*

Pablo smirked. "I wish you hadn't done that, Hailey…" he said.

Hailey grinned. "Why not?" she asked. She had just finished tying her shoes and slowly stood to her feet.

Pablo smiled in return. "I'll tell you guys in the car." He said. "Let's take Shannon and get the hell out of here before Mitch returns."

He picked Shannon up by himself as I helped Hailey toward the door. Hailey's eyes were finally open completely and she seemed to be able to somewhat support her own weight, but she wasn't putting weight on her left foot. That was a concern that could wait until we got into the car. I knew also that it was important that we didn't get caught, especially by Mitch. Trent and Rico were both inherently morons and deserved what they had coming to them. If only Chip, Lynn and Brent could at least be apprehended.

"Don't worry about closing doors." Pablo stated. "They will already know someone was down there anyway, so no use in trying to hide it. When we get out there, we need to get in my car and go."

We had made it up the steps one by one and then made our way back out the side door. So far, the coast was still clear. We were the only ones outside. It kind of puzzled me why the white truck was still here if no one else was around. But then it occurred to me that Mitch drove a black Chrysler 300. So long as we didn't see that, we would be good. *Where's the red convertible?* It occurred to me that the truck may have been Rico's vehicle, and that Trent was not driving his car due to it being easily recognized. As I thought about this, Pablo placed Shannon in the back seat and I helped Hailey into the front seat. Pablo started the car and I moved behind Hailey into the back seat so that I could monitor Shannon.

"I'm glad you had me park like that, Shane." Pablo commented. He wasted no time getting back onto the road from the grass. "We weren't there for more than 25 minutes."

"You will probably pass his car on this road." Hailey mentioned. "He won't give this car a second thought at first… until he gets there and realizes that his warehouse was left wide open."

"Who knows…" Pablo said. "I'm not worried about it."

There was a little bit of silence before Pablo broke it again.

"I had this perfectly schemed…" He said. "In a traditional Virgo fashion."

"Do tell." Hailey and I both said in unison. *Pablo's birthday is September 1.*

"Shannon bought every firearm present in that incident…" Pablo continued. "Under the name Viktoria Romanov. All of them old Soviet design. And… somehow… her Makarov and these MP443's can take the same 9mm rounds, even though they usually don't. Her Makarov was left behind, with only *her* fingerprints on it, because Shane kicked it away. In preparation for this rescue effort, I contacted Hailey's parents and they provided me with Hailey's gun. Shane, last night when you stayed at my place, I swapped the ammo in your magazine for Makarov rounds and did the same with Hailey's, which I was using today. So all five shots fired, from a forensic standpoint, could have come from the Makarov and not our MP443s."

"So, we would have nothing tying us to Trent and Rico's deaths?" I asked.

"Yes…" Pablo started, but then paused, taking a deep sigh and glancing at Hailey. "Except now the project is a little bit contaminated because Hailey decided to take a piss on Trent's corpse and that could put her DNA at the scene of the crime post mortem."

"Not all hope is lost, Pablo…" Hailey said. "Mitch is impulsive. When he gets there he is going to disturb that crime scene beyond recognition. He will be paranoid that his father will see it and he is going to clean everything up and dispose of it all."

Pablo smirked. “And he will make himself a suspect by tampering with the evidence.”

“So, do we know how many bullets are in Shannon’s Makarov right this moment?” I asked. “Because unless its five bullets short and there is residue indicating the gun was fired recently, I think we may have a little bit of a problem with your story.”

“Shannon was doing target practice this morning.” Hailey said. “So her gun *was* fired this morning. And she had an empty magazine sitting on one of the lab tables.”

At least Hailey had the opportunity to witness their daily activities for a few days. Pablo left enough open contingencies in our plan to allow for the uncertainty variables. Some things could just conveniently fall into place and work in our favor.

“Mitch is probably going to tamper with that too…” Pablo continued. “I think we will be fine. There will be enough evidence against them, especially if Mitch cleans up, that I don’t think anyone will even think to do a piss test on Trent’s body.”

“What about Shannon?” I asked. “She is basically the only surviving witness who could, for all intents and purposes, rat us out.”

“I thought about that too…” Pablo continued. “I used one of *her* syringes from HQ on her. So it will wipe her memory leading up to Trent and Rico’s deaths and our escape. The only ones who will have any memory of what really happened back there are in this car and are currently conscious. And… if anyone asks… we broke Hailey free. We will not volunteer any other information. Not even to the media. Is that understood?”

Hailey and I both nodded our heads. Pablo saw my response from the rear view mirror.

“I have a hunch that everything else will fall into place.” Pablo continued. “Including with that machine of theirs. If they ask about the pee? Since they didn't let Hailey relieve herself in a humane fashion, they could have put it in a container and dumped it on Trent. If they ask if they were dead or alive when we got there, there was no one there when we got there. Everything went down after we left. As for everything else, Shannon will incriminate herself with her lack of memory and Mitch's tampering will incriminate him. Banking on the notion that Mitch will sterilize the scene, there is absolutely no way we will be tied to their deaths."

Hailey nodded her head and kept a stoic expression. "So… remind me to never double cross a Virgo."

Pablo and I both chuckled. I reached my arm up and touched Hailey's shoulder. "It's ok, sweetie. This scheme took some heavy devotion… to you."

"I didn't want it to end that way…" Pablo said. "But it was self-defense. If we didn't shoot them first, at least one of us wouldn't be talking right now. And if we didn't kill, we would have left open the possibility of disasters like this happening later on. This is where Mr. McFarlane had it right. It's best to just get the inevitable over with."

"So why did you spare Shannon?" I asked.

"Because having everyone else dead but us would have looked suspicious." Pablo said. "And Shannon surviving, with her battle scars, and no memory. It will be her word against everyone else's. No one will believe her. No one will trust her. She will be as helpless as we were when she had AURORA in a chokehold… and the lives of Shamaya, Randy, and even old George… they will finally have justice."

Hailey chimed in. "Not to mention she is wanted on billboards all across the country." She said. "That will no longer be in her favor."

I nodded my head. "My dad had this saying…" I started. "Don't corner a rat. A cornered animal will fight twice as hard."

"All of us have been cornered for the past two years." Pablo said. "It was just a matter of who was going to have the stamina to survive. We had to bide our time. It's like they say, the cooler heads prevail."

"The war ain't over yet with Bergeron or Mitch still out there…" I said.

"Give it time." Pablo said. "Mitch is next… and we won't even have to do anything. If you are right about him, Hailey, he will self-destruct and take care of himself."

Hailey smiled. "Even with the worst case scenario, I have my full faith and confidence that Troy will work things out for us. We are safe. He isn't the chief but still pretty up there in rank."

Pablo let out a sigh. "So Shane, about your dad…"

I briefly put my hand on his shoulder before sitting back in my seat. "I am sure you had your reasons, Pablo…" I said, giving him a reassuring smile. "I think I already know the answers to my own questions."

"You also know that Shannon was trying to get your goat too, right?" Pablo continued. "I knew his closest friends before the '43 protest rally. People who knew him for years. Corey would never have betrayed those he loved. Besides… it is *also* entirely possible that he was threatened with retaliation if he spoke up about being… taken advantage of."

I nodded my head. "Good point…" I said calmly. "And we both heard those threats from the same mouth. Thank you."

"All good!" Pablo said. He turned to Hailey. "Since we're catching up, what led to them capturing you?"

"I was taking some ferns to Bernice…" Hailey started. "Ran into Shannon's sister. Messaged you. Went to return to my parents stand at Commerce Square and was distracted by a bluebird. I followed it into the forest only to find that Mitch and Shannon set a trap for me. My heel still hurts from their sleep dart. Then… I woke up on that machine."

"What was the purpose of that machine?" I asked. "A dopamine emitter?"

"It was designed to stimulate the pleasure center of the brain." Hailey continued. She started to laugh a little bit. "Specifically using sexual impulses beyond our physiological design… to the point of frying my receptors like an addict's. To their dismay, it wasn't very effective on me. Since things weren't going as planned, I figured all I could do was make the most of it. So I decided to fuck with them. (Laughs) They definitely did not like me showing them up…"

I smiled and reached my hand over the seat and pet Hailey's shoulder. "I've always loved that about you, Hailey…" I said. "Your strong mental discipline. You refuse to be compromised."

Hailey looked back at me with a smile and looked forward again. "Being on the asexual spectrum has its advantages." She said. "They would have had to create a machine specifically for *my* brain's wiring for it to work. You can't use a map of Boston to find your way around Philadelphia."

Pablo nodded his head and smiled. "Your analogy is sound." He muttered.

"I'm glad you understand." Hailey continued. "These deranged people think that they can 'correct' what they perceive as a flaw. My body, and whether or not it is sexually active, is my business. I do not answer to anyone, and I love myself exactly the way I am. And there is so much more to life, and to love, than *getting off*."

I felt my heart flutter as she said those words. "I agree." I said. I caught myself smiling again. "And I love you exactly as you are too."

Hailey glanced back at me with a smile and, with my hand still on her shoulder, she rested her head on it. *I feel like I'm in Heaven with her*.

"Did they bother to feed you at all?" Pablo asked.

"They fed me slop." Hailey said sarcastically. "Probably even *worse* than prison food… but I never lost faith that you guys would eventually find me."

"Maria actually was the one to tip us off…" Pablo said. "Trent's convertible gave away the location. Something that they probably realized too late, given that Trent was there without it."

So I was right about the car. *I suppose this is what happens when you flaunt your goods around for the entire world to see.*

Hailey looked over at Pablo in surprise. "No shit…" she muttered, resting her head on my hand again. "I owe her one."

"We are actually heading to the church…" Pablo continued. "Mr. McFarlane will brief you on what is going on."

I was about to say something when I saw a black Chrysler 300 pass us going the opposite direction. My stomach did a somersault. "Guys, that Chrysler just passed us."

"How far have we driven?" Hailey asked.

"20 kilometers." Pablo said. "Meaning that's how far he has to go before he gets home. We will be long gone."

Hailey smirked. "Hailey 2, Badass wannabees, 0"

The rest of us followed her in laughter as we imagined what kind of fit that Mitch was going to have when he saw that he'd been sacked.

# CHAPTER 13

# A Pyrrhic Victory

We arrived at the church. Gary, Veronica, Mr. McFarlane and Pastor Kevin were waiting for us out front. Pablo and I got out of his car as we parked in front of the church. Hailey got out on her own but was leaning against the car to support her left side. Pablo went to open the rear driver side door to an unconscious Shannon.

"What's she doing here?" Gary asked, readying the stretcher. He was not comfortable with Shannon's presence and had a look of concern.

"She will answer for her crimes..." Pablo said, proceeding to pull her out. Gary helped him place Shannon on the stretcher and then he took her inside.

I looked over to Mr. McFarlane. "Do we have anything to restrain her arms and legs?" I asked. *It's not like she can put up much of a fight with a busted up hand, Shane.*

He smiled. "Of course we do..." he said. "We will worry about that once we're inside."

Veronica walked up to Hailey and gave her a hug. "How are you feeling, doll?"

"I've seen better days…" Hailey joked. "But now that I am returned, better days are also on the way."

Veronica nodded and smiled. "Not a bad way to see it!"

Hailey made an attempt to put weight on her left heel. She winced in pain but was successful. "I… think I may need a brace or something…" she said. She then looked over at me and smiled. "I don't want to be stuck in a hospital bed while Shane goes on the frontlines."

I blushed and put my hand over my face in embarrassment.

"Aww…" Gary had returned just in time to see this. He folded his arms in front of him and grinned at us. "Now that's love!"

"I… just want to be at his side…" Hailey said, smiling at Gary and then at me. She made her way around to the other side of the car where I stood, using the car as a means to support her weight, and fell against me. I was more or less pinned to the car as she put her arms around me and kissed me. I embraced her and felt on top of the world.

Mr. McFarlane cracked a smile. "I'd hate to cut this short, you two, but we need to get inside."

We followed him inside and to the makeshift medical facility in the lower level. Pablo and I helped Hailey walk. It was surprising that she was even able to move after all that she had been through.

"Hailey, my goodness!"

My mom gave Hailey a hug, which she embraced. "I told your parents you were found." she said. "They are out gathering materials for us to help with this makeshift facility, and then they are going to try to help people out on the streets."

"Thank you…" Hailey said softly… holding the hug with my mom. Her eyes were beginning to water.

"Shane!"

I looked over to one of the nearby beds. It was Helen. Her uncle Viktor was at her side. She was sitting up slightly in her bed but holding the side of her that got stabbed. The bandages looked like they had soaked through with blood initially, but the fact that she seemed alert was a great sign for her. I smiled and approached her, attempting to give her a hug from the side of the bed. "It is good to see you aware" I said.

She touched my cheek. "Thank you for saving my life." she said, smiling. I admit that I blushed a little bit when she said this.

"If I didn't know any better, I would deny that you and Shannon were even related…" I said. "You two are seriously night and day!"

Helen laughed. "She's night." she said without missing a beat.

"Speak of the Devil…"

Viktor noticed Shannon's bed being positioned. Her arms and legs were restrained and her right hand was wrapped up. She was awake and did not look happy, but did not seem like she had anything to say to anyone. Helen caught eye contact with the woman who was pushing Shannon's bed and motioned for them to come over.

Shannon's expression was a glare of disapproval. "What are *you* doing here?" she asked.

"Cleaning up your mess…" Helen said sarcastically. "Long time no see, baby sis…"

Shannon looked over at Viktor. "And you too, huh?"

"Consider yourself fortunate that you live in these times." Viktor said. "In my day, the gulags would know you by name."

Shannon smirked. "Not if you know how to negotiate." she said. She looked over at Helen and noticed her wound. "Got into trouble already, I see?"

Helen smiled confidently and smugly kept switching her gaze between Shannon's eyes and her right hand.

"Shut up…" Shannon groaned, putting her head down.

"I think that's enough…" I said. The lady began to roll Shannon away as I turned back toward Helen and Viktor. I shrugged. "I'd hate to see what your family reunions are like…" I joked.

Both of them laughed. I was about to say something when I felt a hand on my shoulder. I turned around to see Pablo standing behind me.

"Mr. McFarlane briefed Hailey on the latest…" he said. "Marco is with our former gang assisting Troy. We need to wait until this *turf war* is over before we head back to HQ and decode that chip. But for now, we can wait here and assist the wounded. Let those in the fights duke it out unless we are called on specifically to help…"

<BEEP!><BEEP!>

Pablo's WCD was receiving a call. "One sec…" he went to answer it. "Talk to me, Marco!"

"Dude, we need backup at the police station, like, now!"

There sounded to be a lot of ruckus in the background. "What's going on?" Pablo asked.

"It's a bloodbath over here, man!" Marco continued. His voice was urgent and rushed. "Two of Bergeron's head officers are going on a rampage and indiscriminately massacring friend and foe alike. They are wiping out the whole fucking building."

"Can you guys withdraw?" Pablo asked.

"I got separated from the group." Marco said. "I am trapped upstairs in the office wing. Anybody going up or down gets shot. The only one that managed to make it with me was Marty from the gang and he is guarding our door. Troy had to take half the team and take it to the streets. Tell Shane not to go home. That neighborhood is a battleground… Gotta go!"

The call ended abruptly as Pablo stood frozen, staring at the counter ticking up on his WCD.

"What's going on?" Mr. McFarlane asked, walking up to both Pablo and I.

"Marco needs backup." Pablo said, looking at Mr. McFarlane. "At the police station."

Both of them looked at me. "I'm still armed…" I said, raising my jacket to reveal my holster. *Am I really volunteering for what is clearly a suicide mission?* I would not have had the grapes to do this before going to New York.

"I'm coming too…"

Hailey made her way over to us walking *mostly* normal. I felt the same vibe from her as the day we met at the protest rally when she voluntarily joined me in the back seat of the police cruiser.

Mr. McFarlane turned to her. "Umm, aren't you in need of some recuperating?" he asked.

Gary and Veronica came up behind her. "She insisted she join Shane's side." Gary said.

"Gary and I made a brace that should last the day." Veronica said, pointing at Hailey's left foot. "Show them, girl!"

Hailey bent down and lifted her left pant leg and there was a metal reinforced cushion brace that she was wearing on her foot.

Mr. McFarlane had an uneasy look toward both of them. "I still don't like this idea." he said.

"Just… let her go…" Pablo said, closing his eyes and putting his hands out in surrender. "We should know by now… if Hailey has her mind made up, nobody can change it but her."

Hailey smirked and directed her eyes in Pablo's direction. I proceeded to make eye contact with her and smile.

Mr. McFarlane sighed. "Very well…" he said. "Follow me outside, you three."

I was about to follow them out when I heard a beckoning from behind me. “Shane, hold on!”

From her hospital bed, Helen was motioning for me to return to her bedside. I stopped next to her and she reached for my hands. “It’s dangerous to go alone.” she said. “Take this.”

Helen placed a small, oddly shaped stone into my hands and gently closed my hands for me as if to secure the stone. It was smooth in texture, shiny, and was nearly pitch black in color. “What is it?” I asked, looking back up at her.

“Black obsidian…” Helen said. “It’s for protection.”

I was confused as to how this could make a difference, but I was going with it. “Anything helps I guess.” I said, smiling. She seemed to know that I knew there was significance in this but I did not yet understand what it was. I eyed the stone for a few seconds and then gently placed it into the right front pocket of my pants. “Thank you.”

“You guys will be safe.” Helen said, smiling reassuringly.

“Shane, you coming?”

Mr. McFarlane had stopped short of the ramp back to the ground level with Hailey and Pablo when he realized that I was not following behind them. I proceeded to sprint in their direction to catch up. We went outside where Mr. McFarlane led us to the back of his van. He opened up one of the back doors and turned toward Hailey. “Shane and Pablo are already armed…” he said, getting a holster and gun ready. “Hailey… mount up!”

Mr. McFarlane handed Hailey the equipment and she proceeded to put it on, albeit a little bit slower than she normally would have. He had a look of concern. “Please… be careful.” he said. “Especially you, Hailey. You aren’t operating on all cylinders right now. If not for the fact that stopping you is a futile effort, I would forbid you from going.”

Hailey smiled. “My apologies in advance for being stubborn…” she said.

--- ---

“Backway as usual.” Pablo said, leading Hailey and I behind him after we parked his car across the street from the police station. This was the same place that we broke into when we stole that airplane back in February. Nothing had changed, except that it was eerily quiet. There was a standing curfew for the public to take shelter and be off of the streets.

“Kind of quiet for a war zone.” Hailey commented as she looked around.

“You guys go in…” Pablo instructed. He stopped and let Hailey and I take the lead. “I am going to find a place to park, and then I am going to try to track down Marco. If anyone points a gun at you, shoot first. If you find Marco first, stay with him.”

I nodded my head and turned around with Hailey. Both of us walked through the corridor. After we had passed through, it shut behind us, blowing a cold wind from outside in the process. Hailey folded her arms in front of her and looked like she wasn’t taking to the climate very well. “This place is giving me the chills…” she muttered.

“Me too…” I added. We started walking down the halls, our footsteps echoing. There were almost no lights on, and the sun was nearly down for the night. The building was all but abandoned. *Late for the party*, I thought. I pulled out my gun and mounted a small tactical flashlight I was carrying in my jacket to the bottom of it. I kicked the light on and began moving it around. We walked slowly down the hall, attempting to be as discreet as possible with our footsteps and the direction I aimed my flashlight.

"So what did Helen need from you?" Hailey asked.

I moved my gun to my left hand as I pulled out the stone from my right pocket. I held it in front of Hailey in the palm of my hand so she could clearly see it. "It's black obsidian. She said it's for protection."

Hailey glanced at the stone and then back up at me. She smiled. "Keep that on you, Shane." she said. "The earth is protecting you."

I placed it back in my pocket. "I guess I don't fully understand." I said.

Hailey took a deep breath, though silently. "Throughout human history, certain objects were believed to have certain… powers. Many ancient cultures in particular believed this. In metaphysics, everything is energy. You. Me. The air. That stone. Helen believes that these *crystals* have such powers, and this one offers protection to whoever bears it."

I nodded my head. "I think I understand now…" I said. "But isn't this like the placebo effect?"

Hailey smiled and gently placed her hand on my shoulder. "Yes." she said. "The placebo effect is proof that our thoughts have the ability to shape reality. If we believe something enough it will have the effects that we expect. Same reason why prayer works. If you believe that this crystal will protect you, then it will. Likewise, if you don't… then it won't. Really it's just an object. A tool for channeling. The real power is in *us*."

This was making some sense. "So that's how you were able to defy physiological science when you were being tortured…" I muttered.

"Kind of..." Hailey continued. "We don't *need* things like this… but it helps to have something tangible to focus on. In my case, my own body served the same purpose. We are all made of the same dust anyway. Not to mention… the same power can be manipulated for ill intent… as Shannon proved."

I nodded my head again. If what Hailey was saying is true, the same forces that gave this crystal its power were also the same forces that led me falling to Shannon's temptations in New York. At Pablo's party I had said that Shannon knew my weaknesses and she would eventually break me down. *Did I manifest that into existence?* I was so afraid of it happening that it happened! *Holy shit*! So that is the importance of controlling one's thoughts. This must also be why my father was so accomplished up until his death. I never knew the man to live in fear. He lived in urgency, yes. If he was afraid, he would not have accomplished even half of what he did. With that being said, my mom's health has greatly improved since she networked with my connections. Living in fear of being alone was killing her. She hasn't been sick in a long while now.

In a sudden movement, I turned the flashlight over to the cells that were now to our right. They were the same cells we were locked up in last year. But something else caught my eye about these. "Hailey, look!"

I stopped in front of a cell and shined my light at a dead body that lay on the ground in there. Whoever it was had curled up into the fetal position before being shot.

"Oh my God…" Hailey said in shock. "You don't think they may have executed all of their prisoners, do you?"

"Well…" I began thinking out loud. "Imagine if you are in charge of a facility. An officer incites an insurrection. What happens when there are more prisoners than cops? And the prisoners take the side of the ones citing the insurrection?"

"Bergeron must've executed them…" Hailey continued. We both looked at each other in horror. "Some of these people were probably innocent, Shane."

I had just noticed that the flashlight was still active on my gun. I left it running. I briefly switched hands again so I could reach into my pocket for the black obsidian and give it a squeeze.

Hailey looked at me with tears in her eyes. "Sorry…" she whispered. She was getting emotional.

I nodded my head and gently pulled her close to me. The sight of death all around us was probably getting to her. "What is it, love?"

"We can talk about it after the mission…" she said. She cleared her throat quietly to try to regain her concentration and we kept moving. About three seconds later, a boom and some screaming could be heard in the distance. I couldn't tell if it was coming from the same floor or the management floor upstairs. Hailey and I quickly began moving our way down to the end of the hall. "Are the floors soundproof?" she asked.

"One would think…" I started. We made it to the front of the isolation ward. I had never been further than this. On the left was another hallway. "The cells we got stuck in last year were holding cells." I explained. "We need to look around down this hall to see if this is the long term."

"It is…" Hailey indicated, pointing at a sign with an arrow on the wall next to the isolation ward's door. "Let's go."

I quickly felt the doorknob to the isolation ward, but it was locked. There was no way we were getting in there. *We're only here for Marco, right*? I thought. I followed Hailey down the hall and shined my light from wall to wall as we proceeded. The further down the hall we got, the more dead bodies there were. I looked over at Hailey, who slowed down her walk and put her hand to her mouth.

"You can even smell the blood…" she pointed out. At the end of the hall was a door leading to the east stairwell of the facility. A dead body lay sitting against the wall, leaning into the corner. But this one looked familiar. I shined my light on him.

"Who does this look like?" I asked. I could somewhat see the face, but the entire left half was covered in blood. He appeared to have a gunshot wound to the chest.

Hailey looked down and spotted an ID badge on him. She pulled it up to herself to read it. "Brent Baier." she read off. Then it hit her. "That's Brent! The one in Trent's group!"

I nodded and continued toward the door to the stairwell. "That's three down..." I said, passing Hailey and anticipating her following me. I didn't give a damn about him. As a matter of fact, as cold as I felt for feeling this way, I felt like rejoicing whenever I had learned of the death of an adversary, even though Brent was the least among them. This was probably not the healthiest response for me to have to the news. The better thing to do would be for me to put it out of my mind. It was interesting that Brent even managed to become an employee of this facility, however short-lived it was.

I held the door for Hailey as she passed through and we made it onto the second floor. We opened the door to bodies. Bodies everywhere, sprawled and laying about randomly in the hallway. It looked like a stereotypical office building up here. Doors and cubicles on each side of us. I gazed my flashlight around all the corpses lying on the floor. Two thirds of them were cops. Others were in street clothes, most notably plain white T-shirts with red bloodstains on them. I looked over at Hailey, who nearly dry-heaved and threw up from the sight of all the carnage. "Keep an eye out for Marco." I said quietly. "Watch your step."

We made our way down the hall, with offices on our left and cubicles on our right. Most of the lights were out, but a few were flickering and buzzing and offering just enough light to where we could navigate without tripping over the cesspool. We passed a break room on our left. *I could really use a coffee about now*, I thought.

"What is it?" Hailey asked. She appeared to have seen my facial expression. I hadn't realized that I almost laughed there.

"I was just thinking…" I started. It was no use hiding the funny idea now. A smile cracked across my face. "It's been a long day. A cup of coffee sounds pretty good right now."

Hailey gave me her *Pisces Eyes* and lightly jabbed me in the shoulder. "Not now, Shane." She said quietly. She appeared to be trying not to crack a smile, but I could tell it was hard for her to fight it off. This probably was not the appropriate time for that.

We stopped at the end of the hall where we could either go left or right. The right was much shorter and only contained a few offices. The left looked like it had around 15 rooms, all on the left wall and windows on the right wall. I led the way.

"This is surreal…" Hailey said quietly. "And to think this place was vibrant only two days ago."

"A lot can happen in an instant." I mentioned. There were a few conference rooms mixed in with a copy room and another break room. We got to the 6th door when I heard a cough and a groan coming from the door that we had just passed. I stopped, and Hailey stopped right behind me. We both looked at each other.

"Did you hear that?" I asked. Hailey nodded her head yes. She had the look of fear in her eyes and her breathing looked to be a little more labored now.

We both turned around and entered the room. It looked to be an administration office. Against the right wall was a bookcase. Before I could observe any further, I heard someone whisper my name. The voice was weak and strained. I looked over and gasped at who it was.

"Marco!"

Hailey and I ran over to his side. "He's bleeding badly, Shane…" Hailey mentioned. I stood up for a moment and took a look around the room to see if anyone else was around. There were two older men lying dead behind the desk. Their name tags read "Rodney" and "Turley".

These were the same two officers that were present when we got locked up after the debates. It appeared that Marco won this gunfight… just barely.

"I… can feel myself going…" Marco struggled to say. He moved his left hand slightly to reveal a gunshot wound he received to the chest. He was breathing heavily, and had a small stream of blood dripping from the edge of his mouth. "Was… there anyone else alive?"

"I'm afraid not…" Hailey muttered. She set her WCD to record the conversation. "You are the first sign of life we've seen since we got here."

Marco looked away for a moment. "Damn…" he said weakly. "Marty… all of them… I'm the last one."

I quickly reached for my WCD. "Pablo. I found Marco. 2nd floor in the admin office. He's critical."

"On my way." Pablo said. "Tell him to hang in there for me. Outer perimeter is clear."

The call terminated and Marco continued.

"We heard of Troy's insurrection… I got in touch with Bigelow… rounded up some of the old gang and we stormed the doors. I told the rest of the baseball team to stay home and protect their neighborhoods, so it was just me and the gang. The officers used the security alarm as a signal… to open fire. It was us against officers… and officers against other officers. Through all this, some escaped, including Bergeron. These two… mowed down everyone alive. Indiscriminately…"

Marco's speech was interrupted by a rogue cough, which subsided after about ten seconds. "Seeing their rampage, I hid in here… trapped… waiting for them to turn their backs. But they never did. They found me and…"

He looked like he was having trouble staying conscious. I offered him support and repositioned him to where it was less strain on his body. “Stay with us, Marco…” I begged of him. “At least wait for Pablo to find his way here...”

“I don’t know, man…” Marco said desperately. I had a bad feeling that this was going to be the last hurrah from him. “Whatever you guys do… find Bergeron. And make him strike out. Make… him… strike…”

*[Scene slows to slow motion - Queue song: Elliot Smith - Everything Means Nothing to Me]*

His last three words were spoken slower and softer than the rest of everything he had said. This was a visual that I knew would never leave me. He was looking right at Hailey and I at the beginning of that sentence. In those last three words, his eyes appeared to lose focus and his head slowly turned to the side. The rest of his body followed in going limp. Marco had just passed away.

In our moment of shock, Hailey and I looked up to see Pablo just now arriving in the doorway. He read the looks on our faces quickly. An expression of despair ensued. He walked into the room and crouched in front of Marco, effectively splitting Hailey and I to where now we were both at Pablo’s sides. Hailey’s eyes began to water and she put her hand to her mouth. Pablo took the stopwatch he wore around his neck into the palm of his hand. “This is the last fucking time I am going to be late for anything!” he told himself. There was a hint of anger in his tone. He clutched the stopwatch as if he was going to crush it with his bare hands.

“He was…” Pablo started talking, but he choked up and buried his face in his hands. “... He was my brother, man…” he cried.

I had never seen Pablo outright cry like this. My heart broke for him. Hailey and I both looked at each other. We knew what to do. The both of us stood up and put our hands on either side of Pablo and began praying for him, as well as for Marco and all the chaos of the past few days. The three of us proceeded to grieve together for Marco Rodriguez. When Hailey told Pablo that she recorded his last words, that paved the way to make his heroic deeds known in that the prison massacre ended with him.

## CHAPTER 14

# Turning the Tide

### *(Earlier that day)*

Mitch pulled into his driveway and made a beeline for the side door of the barn upon exiting the car. He reached for his keys only to find that the padlock was not even on the door. *Fuck!* He hastily opened the door and saw that most of the interior of the barn was untouched, but that the storm doors to the lower level were left wide open. "God damnit!"

He made his way down and rushed through the cellar, starting to panic. The keypad controlled door was also left open. "Yo, Trent? Rico?"

Mitch's call for his *League* allies went unanswered. He continued to the final room where the main lab and the torture machine were located. "Is anyone down here?" he shouted. "Shannon?"

As Mitch made his way to the corner, he could smell the stench of blood and discharged firearms. He spotted Rico's corpse adjacent to the machine and Trent's in front of it. In the midst of his panic, the smell of urine barely registered on his senses as he assumed that Trent's body released it upon his demise.

"Shannon?" He shouted. The room was eerily silent except for the sound of a mainframe computer running closer to the entrance. Five 9mm bullet casings lay on the floor near where he stood. He pulled out his cellphone and attempted to dial Chip, nearly fumbling the keys as he typed.

"Come on, man. Answer!" Mitch shouted. It rang four times and went to voicemail. He made an attempt to call Lynn.

*"The owner of the number you have dialed has been apprehended by the Winchester Police department. If you wish to contact this phone subscriber directly, please contact the Winchester Police department during business hours at..."*

Mitch hung his phone up and leaned against the wall, ultimately sinking to the floor into a sitting position. He knew that he was on his own, and that the rest of his cohorts had either been picked up or killed in the upcoming turf war. Brent was no longer in the League, having been "promoted" to working at the police station itself under Bergeron, so contacting him was out of the question.

"Welp, I guess it's up to me, then..." Mitch muttered to himself, standing back up to his feet. He made his way into the pantry where he pulled two body bags from his stock to put Trent and Rico into. One by one he pulled his two fallen comrades up the cellar steps and onto the barn's ground level. He then took them to the back and laid them both next to each other. He wasn't sure what to do with them and would need to figure it out the next day, as his dad would be home from work in less than two hours and he would have to act nonchalant about his activities of the day.

Mitch made his way back down to the cellar and gathered the necessary materials to clean up the blood and any stains from the perimeter. Given that everything within the vicinity was made out of cement, glass or metal, the effort did not take very long. Within the next hour he had everything picked up as normal, but little did he know that he was simply prolonging the inevitable.

*(Mitch's warehouse, the next day. 12:00pm)*

"What the fuck is this, Mitch?"

Gerald Cantrell returned home to scold his son. Stories were pouring in on the morning news of the previous evening's events. He had gone to work in the morning only to have the company's board members confront him, and then vote to send him home. Gerald had felt humiliated by the event. The sudden coverage of the events at the police station had blindsided him, and although he had nothing to do with it, his indirect involvement via Officer Bergeron had made him a target. Mitch was sitting in a fold out chair at one of the lab tables, slouching and avoiding direct eye contact. Gerald stood in the doorway.

"What is what, dad?" Mitch asked. His behavior emulated that of a belligerent teenager.

"That fucking device against the wall over there!" Gerald shouted, pointing at the torture machine that was used on Hailey. He got close enough to be in Mitch's face, but lowered his voice and remained sharp with his tone. "Had I known that this was going to be the business that you were conducting when I was not around, I would *never* have willed this place to you!"

Mitch shrugged. "So what!" he snapped back condescendingly. "I was helping Shannon accomplish her goal of attaining freedom."

"Leave that to *me*!" Gerald growled, briefly pointing at himself. "You were told to help *take them down*. Not *torture* them! *THIS* is not called for! Unless I've got it wrong. Tell me I'm wrong, and I will let up."

Mitch could not find the words to say at the moment, which aroused his father's suspicion.

"I thought so." Gerald continued. He already knew the answer to the questions that he was about to ask. He just wanted to see if his son would lie to him about it. "I am only going to ask you this once. What is it? And what is its purpose?"

Mitch smiled. "Would you refuse to answer if you knew you were only going to be asked the question once?" he asked.

Gerald slammed his fist on the table to startle him. "Don't get smart with me, Mitch!" He shouted. "I told you I was only going to *ask* once! Now, I am DEMANDING an answer!"

Mitch glanced at the machine and looked back toward Gerald again. "It's designed to control dopamine." He said. "More specifically, using the body's sexual impulses beyond natural parameters to cause dopamine floods. To get them hopelessly addicted and to eventually fry their receptors like a drug addict."

Gerald nodded his head. "I see…" he said. "And you had someone down here?"

"Kind of…" Mitch muttered.

"That is a yes or no question, Mitch." His father growled.

"Shannon used it for fun." Mitch continued. "But we did use the machine on one of AURORA's members."

"And where is she now?" Gerald asked.

Mitch paused for a moment. "Gone…" he said. "She either escaped or someone came here and broke her free."

"Meaning your victim is at large and someone on the outside is aware of this... contraption." Gerald said. "On *my* property."

He turned around and grabbed a remote control hanging in a cradle on the wall behind him. He then turned back toward Mitch and shook it in his right hand as he spoke. "You know what happens if the media finds out that *my son* is sexually torturing a woman in *my* basement? Bad press! Let me show you."

Gerald pushed a button on the remote control and a large projector TV lowered itself at the opposite wall. The device kicked on as soon as it had been fully deployed. He changed the channel to the local news.

*"The last 24 hours have left the town in shock as tragedy struck at the county police station. It all started when the station was stormed by an alliance of gangs, who then teamed up with a group of police officers that were citing an insurrection against police chief Reginald Bergeron. A bloodbath ensued inside of the police station before the battle was taken outside and occupied many residential neighborhoods on the south side. At least 86 law enforcement employees and civilians alike are dead and 268 more confirmed wounded. Some local residents have volunteered their time at Winchester District Christian Church to treat the wounded, as the Northside Hospital has reached its capacity."*

*[Interviewing: John McFarlane - Teacher at Winchester High (Ret.)]*

*"This is one of those things that you hope you never have to live to see it happen in your town. But when it does, it almost feels like a civic duty to find out what you can do to help."*

*[Returns back to the news reporter]*

*"The officer that cited the insurrection claims that Officer Bergeron has sexually molested several women in his more than 20 year career and has been known to abuse his power. Since this accusation was made known this morning, more than 25 residents have called the studio and came forward with their story in the last five hours alone. At this time, no one was available for comment at the police station, and Bergeron's whereabouts are also unknown, as he has allegedly fled Winchester following the accusations brought against him. What remains of the police force are out on street patrol, both the rebels and those loyal to the police chief. There were no survivors in the station itself. This is the story for now. Channel 6 news."*

Gerald turned the TV off and tossed the remote onto the lab table. He gave Mitch a stern look. "*That*, son, is WHY we need to stay out of this… Hopeless Media." he barked. "Once someone digs *any* dirt on you, it *is* hopeless! Miss Boyer may have been trying to repay her debts, but my collaboration with Bergeron was both a civic duty and a business deal. And thanks to you, it's been FUCKED!"

He hauled off and backhand slapped Mitch hard enough to knock him out of his chair and onto the ground. Mitch lay on his side holding the left side of his face, gazing back to his father with a surprised look of fear.

"Your sadism has cost me!" Gerald continued. "WE could be next if that tortured girl were to say anything, enemy of the state or not! What were you thinking? The public is going to look at her like a hero for trying to expose us! And then what? What about the company? Bad press. Dropped stocks. Actually… The public finding out about this could drive the board to face my resignation! So, Mitch, congratulations. Thanks to you, I have to cut ties with Bergeron. That business deal is *gone*. And you are worse for the company's publicity than Miss Boyer *ever* was! And I could be out of a job!"

He turned around to storm back through the corridor, but stopped at the doorway. He turned back around to face Mitch one more time. "Oh, and I am changing the combination to the keypad. Go back to the house. NOW!"

Mitch slowly got up and reluctantly followed his father out. Revenge. Payback for betrayal. Those were the things on his mind as he walked out the door.

--- ---

Hailey and I were walking back from the church, which was just past my mom's work. It was about 3:00 in the afternoon and we were on our way back to my house. Every street corner had a cop on patrol. They had spent the entire morning cleaning up the bodies, although it wasn't nearly as severe as at the police station. Much of the neighborhood had been evacuated due to yesterday's skirmish, but for the most part, the police that were here did a fantastic job of making things look like they never happened. Fortunately, the temperature was still about 11 degrees Celsius. No snow to retain blood stains, and vegetation was minimal since it was out of season. This year had pretty much been an Indian summer so far. It was the warmest December on average that I had seen in years.

We approached our part of the street. Since the neighborhood was supposed to be clear now, the OK was given for us to see if we could clean up the mess left in my house from when it was ransacked. A trip to the store was necessary also, as I was certain any perishable items in the fridge were spoiled by now.

"How've your parents been?" I turned to Hailey and asked. "Did you tell them what happened?"

"I did…" she said. "I called the news station to finally report my case with being raped by Bergeron. It was followed by countless others calling the station as well. I think we have him where we want him."

"My mom called as well…" I continued. "Better late than never."

"I hope they find his ass…" Hailey muttered. "At least this has had the side effect of Mitch's dad's company tanking. So he is in some deep shit now too."

"I think that is why Pablo said not to mention the torture device." I said. I paused for a moment and glanced at Hailey. "You *didn't* mention that to the media, right?"

Hailey smiled. "Of course not!" she said. "I trust Pablo as much as you do. It sounds like he knew that this matter would take care of itself on its own. Hell, I wouldn't put it past Mr. Cantrell to turn on his own son to save his stake in that company."

"I could totally see that..." I said. "If things *did* go according to plan, Mitch will probably be desperate and unhinged. Like the cornered rat. We best be careful."

I was about to show her that I was still armed when a tall, uniformed police officer approached us from the left. He stood at about 188 centimeters. He seemed calm and gazed over at us with an expression that indicated that he just wanted to talk. We stopped and waited for him. "What are you two up to?" he asked.

"Hailey and I are just going back to my house." I explained, pointing in the direction of my house just ahead. "It got ransacked and she was going to help me clean it up."

He nodded his head, but had a look like he knew something. "Conliffe?"

Hailey and I looked at each other and then back to the officer again. "Yes." I responded. "Shane Conliffe."

"Bigelow." The officer reached out his hand with a smile to shake mine. "Troy Bigelow."

We shook hands and then he proceeded to shake Hailey's. "We've met..." he said, laughing.

"I was hoping to meet you eventually…" I said. *This guy seems pretty cool*. "I heard a lot about you but was told it was dangerous with Bergeron around. We didn't want to blow your cover."

"Thanks for that!" Troy said coolly. "Your father and my father both knew each other. So I think it is only right that you and I finally get to know one another."

"We also heard about you from John McFarlane." Hailey said. "You were also *friends* with Muhammad for the short time he worked at the station."

He quickly looked around us on all sides as if to check the perimeter and then bent down a little bit to make sure that his voice didn't travel when he was talking to us. "Yeah… about that…" Troy started. "That chip has Bergeron's history. Those people that came forward today about being sexually assaulted? Those aren't new. He hid the cases on the computer to where no one could see them and then locked them as classified. Only his computer could unlock them. Muhammad was brilliant at getting these files raw. The chip was the only thing he could write to without it setting off a security alarm because of how obsolete it is. (Turns to me). If you have the means to decode that chip, I can guarantee that you will have the hard evidence to *convict* Bergeron."

Hailey and I both smiled. The idea of having possession of all of this, with the potential of taking down someone who was more or less an untouchable politician, was exciting to me. *Now we have an idea of what's on the chip*, I thought.

"You guys should make it quick." Troy said. "In fact, let me escort you if that is ok. There are still a few loose cannons out here."

"Thank you…" I said. This works out perfectly. I didn't want a repeat of what happened when I had Helen with me. "Last time I tried to enter my house, someone was there preventing me from being able to enter."

The three of us headed to my house. I went to unlock the door and I heard a sound come from the inside of the house.

"Guys , hold up…" Troy started, drawing his gun. "I heard something. Open the door and stand off to the side. Leave the doorway clear."

Hailey ducked and went to the left side of the door and Troy to the right. I unlocked the door and quickly opened it, immediately jumping onto Hailey's side.

<POP!><POP!>

Whoever was in there fired two shots, but both just went right out the front door. It was a good thing that none of us were standing in front of the door when I opened it.

Troy wrapped his arm around the doorway and fired a shot into the house. "FREEZE!" he shouted "POLICE! COME OUT WITH YOUR HANDS UP!"

He stepped in front of the doorway with his gun drawn. Whoever was inside fired a third shot, striking Troy, but he didn't fall. Troy let another shot of his own go.

"AHH, GOD DAMNIT!"

Troy ran into the house and Hailey and I followed to back him up. All three of us had our guns drawn. "DROP THE WEAPON!" Troy shouted. He reached for the receiver on his walkie-talkie. "Shots fired at 3853 Roseberry St. Suspect is wounded and I took one to the vest. Requesting backup to help take him into custody."

"10-4"

The guy was none other than Mitch. "You two…" he muttered, recognizing both Hailey and I.

"Surprise!" Hailey taunted.

"You faggots had to get a cop?" Mitch sneered. He sat up holding his left shoulder.

"Mind your slurs…" Troy said, leaning down and flipping Mitch over with his foot. "I happen to swing that way."

He proceeded to put Mitch in handcuffs, apprehending him.

"Wait a minute…" Mitch muttered. He was refusing to face or make eye contact with any of us. "Did you just admit that you're gay?"

"Don't ask questions you don't want to know the answer to." Troy said, getting Mitch onto his feet. "You have the right to remain silent. Anything you say can and will be used against you in a court of law.

You have the right to an attorney. If you do not have one, one will be provided to you by the state."

Hailey and I looked at each other. There would be no judgment from either of us. But this display from Troy was pure professionalism. That is exactly what we would want in our next police chief.

"Please…" Mitch pleaded.

"After the torture that you tried to put me through?" Hailey taunted. "Dream on…"

"Why you bitching?" Mitch asked. "You probably benefited from it. Pussy boy here will probably thank me for it later."

His remark was of course directed at me. But all I could do was smirk. He was not in a position to assert his dominance.

"You won't last long in prison, buddy…" Troy said sarcastically. "I suggest you don't drop the soap."

I turned to Hailey, who had her hand to her mouth giggling at Troy's comment. "Please tell me that someone has something they can knock him out with…" I said. "A blackout syringe. Anything?"

"You guys don't need to worry about it." Troy said. He directed Mitch toward the front door. "I am taking him outside. You guys assess what you need to do here."

"Thanks officer." Hailey and I both said in unison.

As Troy headed out the door and closed it behind him, we both looked at each other and then took a look around. There were a couple of stray bullet holes peppered about the room. A broken vase that was to the right of the stairs lay with its contents spilling onto the floor. The place needed work but nothing that I could see was officially missing.

"I guess it could've been worse…" I muttered, shrugging my shoulders.

Hailey looked over at me. "Now that Mitch is in custody, we should probably see about reconvening with everyone at HQ." she said. "The threat has been neutralized."

I looked over toward the stairwell. "I did have a reason to come here..." I started, making my way over to remove the panel. I proceeded to pull out one of my father's totes. "If I am not mistaken, I think I recall my dad's Windows 10 laptop having some kind of code breaker software. We need to get *this* to HQ."

I pulled out a 2016 era Dell laptop and its power adapter and proceeded to put everything else back into its place. I made my way to my room and Hailey followed. "Time is of the essence..." I said, grabbing my empty school backpack from against the wall in front of my bed. The laptop and power adapter fit perfectly into the bag.

"Well, shall we?" Hailey asked, smiling.

I smiled back. "We shall..." I said, swinging the backpack over my shoulder.

She pecked a kiss at me and we proceeded to leave for HQ.

# CHAPTER 15

# Unfinished Business

*January 2046*

All of us as a group ended up attending the funeral for Marco Rodriguez two days after Christmas. The entire baseball team was there in support. When Pablo went up to speak, he prayed that this would be the last time that we would have to bury a friend, but that Marco was a hero. Marco had money that he was saving up during his time as a ball player, and he ended up willing it toward the medical care of those injured in the turf war. Just prior to meeting with the old gangs at the police station, he had notarized the will officially at the local bank, knowing that he had the chance of not making it out of there alive. "He was just as good at covering his bases as he was throwing to them" Pablo had said. After the funeral, Hailey and I suggested that we could try to come up with something that will allow locals to remember him, but that we would give him space first. Mr. McFarlane temporarily assumed his role in AURORA to give Pablo time for bereavement after having lost one of his best friends. Maria was fast at his side as well. I never would have thought that she of all people would be where she is today, but it seems that a lot can change in two years.

At the turn of the year, the church was still being used to assist the injured, but slowly things were clearing out. The Northside Hospital had managed to ship supplies and even a few personnel over to assist us after Mr. McFarlane was interviewed by Channel 6 again, and progress was finally being made. There were 49 people left and 16 were looking to go home today. I wasn't much of a medical person, nor did I bring any useful knowledge to the table, but even just running errands I was content with being some part of this. The municipalities of the town were in disarray, but the police station was able to regroup and Troy Bigelow has become the interim police chief for the time being, with official elections being held later this year. A majority of the people I have talked to seem to have their full faith and confidence in him, myself included. Hailey, my mom and I assessed the damage in my house and we were able to clean everything up. To our amazement, everything was accounted for. A few things were vandalized but nothing was missing.

We waited until the second week of the New Year to reconvene at HQ as a group. I had spent a lot of time running the decoding algorithm on the MicroSD card, but would not be able to access all of the data until all of it was decoded. Two decades of data was understandably going to take time to decode, especially when the task was being performed by a 30 year old laptop. It had finally finished a few nights ago and I had put everything away to give the computer a rest before today's presentation.

*MCFARLANE, JOHN C. --APPROVED.*

*BURNETT, HAILEY S. --APPROVED.*

*CONLIFFE, SHANE R. --APPROVED.*

*CLOVER, GARY F. --APPROVED.*

*NOLAN, VERONICA N. --APPROVED.*

*CONLIFFE, PATRICIA A. --APPROVED.*

In a rare exception, Mr. McFarlane allowed Helen and Viktor, who had remained in town for the time being, to enter without signing in. They had been a huge help to our cause, and also saw Shannon off as she was prepping to be transported to a high security prison somewhere out west. No exchange of words was needed between them. Their facial expressions explained it all. Shannon with her resentment and vengefulness, and Helen and Viktor with their unsurprising disapproval of her. Pablo remained at his house with Maria on what could be considered leave. At one point, I asked Veronica why she didn't take leave when Shamaya was killed and she said it was her choice to do so at the time. She was given the option but she was driven to press on. Pablo wasn't known for his clear expression of emotion and recent events had broken him.

I sat at Randy's old desk and Hailey sat where Shannon used to sit. Gary and Veronica sat on the couch that was against the back wall. Helen and Viktor sat at the one adjacent to the left. My mom and Mr. McFarlane sat at the one closest to the kitchen. That meant 3 out of 4 couches had people sitting in it for the first time since the 2044 elections. The only one that was vacant was the one closest to our work desks.

"Alright, let's get started!" Mr. McFarlane said, standing up. "So here is the latest. We have determined Muhammad Al-Alawi's cause of death. The autopsy indicated that he succumbed to cardiac arrest, and the toxicology report showed traces of fentanyl in his system. My guess is that he was the target of a micro syringe and made a mad dash toward Commerce Square before he would be too delirious to reach us. However… his efforts were not in vain. Thanks to Shane and Helen we not only found him, but his overall mission with Troy Bigelow has succeeded as well, as we are now in possession of the information he intended to deliver to us."

There were some affirming glances being directed in both my direction and in Helen's. Mr. McFarlane continued.

"I would also like to thank Patricia, Gary, Veronica, and even Helen and Viktor for helping out with the makeshift medical facility. Even to Hailey's parents. Our community found these services to be a blessing. (Turns to Hailey and I) And you two… (Sighs) I am sorry that you guys have been through hell and back, but damn it all if you didn't come back smelling like a rose. Doing some of the dirty, frontline work. Thanks to you guys and Pablo's direction, I mean… it would seem that our adversary's stronghold is all but crippled. Now all that is left to do is to see what exactly was on that chip. Shane, if you would do the honors!"

I pulled out the laptop and proceeded to plug it in on the work desk. I then took my dad's old WCD and its USB adapter and connected that. Finally, I took the MicroSD card and put it in the WCD.

"Are you able to connect that to the projector?" Mr. McFarlane asked. All eyes were on me at this point but I was confident enough in how to use this equipment that I didn't mind the pressure.

"It has HDMI" I said. I unplugged a cord from the back of the main computer and plugged it into the side of the laptop. I lowered the projector with a button on the desk and it came to life.

"I wonder what we are going to see…" Hailey muttered.

"We will soon find out." I said, anticipating what was going to show up. The projection was on the back wall above the couch that Gary and Veronica were sitting on. I went into the menu on the laptop and located my dad's software. It had just occurred to me how my dad got a hold of this. I turned to Mr. McFarlane. "I think I figured it out, guys!" I started. I turned my chair toward the group so I could be better heard. "My dad, being friends with Troy's father Norm, was able to get not just *a* working piece of software. This is *the* software! As in, the actual shit they are using at the station even today! Norm snagged him a legit copy of Bergeron's encryption software before he quit!"

A smirk came across Mr. McFarlane's face. It must have been why he waited until the next day to resign after my mom's incident. "Well, I'll be damned…" He turned toward the rest of us. "Looks like Randy wasn't the only one who has been helping us posthumously. Both Norm and Corey were getting their paws dirty too."

Hailey chimed in. "Randy managed to write entire manuals on how to operate the equipment here." she said. "Which was on a similar card that Veronica found hidden in the desk. Shannon had considered herself irreplaceable by keeping her skills to herself. But she was out so much that Randy had time to figure things out for himself."

Gary turned to Veronica. "It's all coming together now, ain't it?!"

"Holy shit, guys!" I called out. I opened the software and proceeded to access the card's now decrypted data. On the screen displayed cases going back to 2025 of allegations against Bergeron. Official ones. They had encrypted and buried them. There were over 200 files, and that was just against Bergeron. "200 files against Bergeron… several against this Gerald Cantrell guy…"

"That's Mitch's father…" Hailey said. "And evidently the one who was responsible for making Shannon an enemy of the state. It was *his* medical convention that she crashed in 2041."

"Backup *all* of it!" Mr. McFarlane suggested. "I am going to set up a distribution to the news media to report it, and perhaps even send this to the President of the United States himself. Let's get this show moving!"

Cheers and clapping filled the room as we felt the need to celebrate victory. Of course, there was still a lot of work to do, but we had the hard evidence to put away all of those responsible for making the lives of the locals miserable. At least, the ones that survived the turf wars.

As time went on, Mr. McFarlane was able to send the information to the proper authorities for processing. Hailey and I would visit HQ to make sure everything was working properly. After we were done with the MicroSD card, I put that, my dad's WCD and that old laptop back in its tote underneath the stairs at my house. Gary and Veronica were working side jobs while attending the university, but both of them were inspired to take on Criminal Justice and responded to a help wanted ad at the police station posted by Troy. They were successfully interviewed and Troy took both of them under his wing. They went back to being only part time members of AURORA once again, but they were able to keep their WCDs, much in the same way my mom is a member. All of us congratulated them and told them how proud we were of their desire for justice and making a difference. In the end, you don't have to be part of some political activist group to do it. Both of them were excited to do their part in revitalizing the community that had been crippled for so long under Bergeron's reign.

Viktor had returned with Helen back home to Arizona with her family, and some of us were able to keep in touch with them as friends. The hospital had taken in the remainder of the patients that were at the church and my mom and I worked on fixing the damage to our house. Hailey and her parents decided to help make things look more "aesthetically pleasing to the eye" in the aftermath of our neighborhood becoming a war zone. The turf wars actually ended up benefiting their business, although they refused to charge customers whose work was in relation to that. This didn't stop people from donating, however. It was almost like community homeowners insurance.

Although he was already performing the duties of the seat, Troy Bigelow had been *officially* promoted to interim police chief until emergency elections were to be held in the Spring. The dirt we found on Bergeron was going to end up locking up half of the town hall for racketeering and embezzlement, but we weren't going to act on it until we had all of the information at once. It was no wonder he was so powerful and that he had the police under his thumb. He had a ton of connections even outside of the community where ill money funneled in. Muhammad managed to capture that information too! We were going to try to report everyone and everything that we could to the media, but we were going to have them start with the locals first. It was going to be interesting to see if the state was going to step in, or if these positions would end up on the emergency election as well.

By the end of January, we had found that there were close to a dozen officials in the town hall that had ties to Bergeron's corruption. The accused council members refused to leave office, but as the story of Bergeron became more widespread and was aired on national news, criticism and discontent of the status quo became more common. They attempted to legislate their way back into control, but Officer Bigelow's efforts to turn around the reputation of the police force was successful, and they found that they could not enforce the ordinances that they were putting in place.

While this was going on, President Barr had continued working with congress to reverse the tyrannical actions of the presidents that preceded him going back at least 20 years. In that year's State of the Union speech, Barr had mentioned our town by name and called out Reginald Bergeron for his antics, and then proposed re-evaluating the "enemy of the state" law and giving everyone who had their lives ruined as a result of it a "fair trial". He had indicated that each scenario would be a case by case basis and that while some were indeed treasonous conspirators, others were blacklisted simply for exercising their first amendment rights. This was absolutely a step in the right direction.

CHAPTER 16

# Emergency Elections

In February, four more of the council members had been forced to resign and the state had appointed interim members to stay until the emergency elections. Hailey had suggested that Mr. McFarlane run for one of the vacant positions. Given that he was riding on positive publicity in assisting with the injured a few months ago, he figured "Why not". He kickstarted a campaign that did not require much funding, and instead of touring and giving speeches, he volunteered in community service activities. He ran on the premise "Why talk the talk, when you can walk the walk?" This started a movement with the entire community coming together to assist one another in cleaning up blight, landscaping, food drives and the like. Some of the other board members that were trying to escape the media's grip tried to follow suit, but were constantly reminded of their dirt and were dismissed as "copycats". By the end of the month, there were not enough council members to run the city beyond a skeleton crew and much of the town had been running on emergency management.

On March 1, Officer Bergeron had finally been arrested in Baltimore in what appeared to be the home base of an even bigger multi-national organization of corruption. Not having the power to do this himself,

President Barr urged communities across the nation to "clean house" of those involved and hold new local elections to replace the vacancies. While he could not order this organization closed, or a cease and desist, to date he had been looking for people who knew their way around technology that would make it more difficult for such an organization to operate. Or, at the least, become like "Anonymous" was in the 2010s and have a special "hacktivist" group to target them. I kind of had issues with what Barr was pushing, but didn't complain much because it fit my mold. My mom told me that my dad would have pointed out that this view would have made me a part of the problem. Regardless, I did feel as bad as the next guy. Mr. McFarlane had told me that what I was seeing from Barr was the result of a "bandwagon", and every candidate and politician had theirs in every era of the United States of America. This country was always like this in some form or another, just that the demographics with the advantages and disadvantages changed with each era. It was our guess that whoever was going to take such a job would be coordinating with the FBI or CIA, as they have been involved in these matters for nearly a century now.

## *March 30, 2046*

*[Channel 6 News]*

*"City council has eight new members today as a result of yesterday's emergency elections. Of these, the one that has taken the community by storm has to be John McFarlane."*

*"McFarlane has a long history. He first served our country in the first Gulf War in 1991, and then later on again in Iraq in 2003. He would retire after 20 years in the service to become a high school history teacher, becoming a mentor to some and a hard knocks instructor to*

*others. He would teach both civics and world history for 33 years at Winchester High School before retiring last year."*

*"He ran his campaign on 'why talk the talk, when you could walk the walk', and spent his time serving the community instead of giving speeches. This was a brilliant form of self-promotion that has always been hard to find in today's politics. The people have been itching for public servants in office rather than politicians, and I think that proves this point."*

A TV was on in the corner of the office as I was helping Mr. McFarlane set up in the town hall. This was something that I never thought that I would see. As the news had stated, he had a very extensive career, and it was exciting to see him move to the next big thing. He was tough as nails, and I felt that he deserved this. He has spent his long life doing nothing but serving others and taking the time out to help people. I didn't even know that he had a family until recently, although he always kept his personal life extremely private. He was married at one time, but his wife passed away from cancer in 2036. It had occurred to me that his serving others was likely therapeutic to him. I couldn't imagine the loneliness of having that kind of personal life. Or lack thereof.

"How do you move from one thing to the next?" I asked, setting down a cardboard box of files against the wall.

"Two words, Shane." he said, as he was rearranging books on a bookshelf. A trophy for a boxing championship in 2004 was positioned in front of a few of these books on a high shelf. "Stay active."

He turned toward me and continued talking. "The moment you get lazy… the moment you shut down your mind… your body is going to shut down with it. I'm old, but it takes a mirror to convince me that I am a day over 40..."

"Which is how old you were at the beginning of your last journey." I pointed out.

He smiled and chuckled under his breath. "I never would've thought I would have been a teacher that long. Heck, I wasn't even going for 33 years. I was thinking maybe 20 or so. But, as difficult as they were… My best years were the final ones. Meeting you, Hailey, and the others."

"I am glad that Hailey had you run for this office." I said. "It is great to see you do so much with your life."

Mr. McFarlane nodded his head and stared out the window behind his desk from in front of the bookcase. "We have to make the most out of the life we're given." he said. A bluebird flew by the window and then landed on the branch of a tree outside. He let out a sigh and continued talking. "Shannon had such potential too… but ended up succumbing to her darkness. I was a naive fool with her."

"You had good intentions." I reassured. "She had everyone fooled, not just you. But look at where she is at and look where we are at!"

He continued speaking. "I had thought that *my* potential was gone after I retired from teaching. I am not much of a public speaker, which is why I didn't tour that long giving motivational speeches. I am a doer, not a talker, Shane. (Turns toward me) As you saw… I hope to continue that till the day I die."

He smiled and then I smiled back. We were almost done carrying the last of his stuff from the back of his van. He headed toward his office door and I followed. As we reached the hallway, his phone began to go off. "It's a private number." He muttered.

I nodded my head and stood off to the side. He proceeded to lead us back into his office.

"John McFarlane speaking."

"Guess who's coming back to town?"

Mr. McFarlane stopped in his tracks. He glanced back at me with a look of shock and then faced forward again. "Robert! It is so great to hear from you! I thought that you were still undercover."

"Well, I'm wrapping up." Robert said. "Turns out that I have been given the all clear. The recent shakeup in Winchester had a domino effect on my end. Whatever happened there resulted in me being honorably discharged from this particular duty."

"Are you free to talk about it?" Mr. McFarlane asked.

"Not yet." Robert continued. "But soon enough. I will be in town next week."

"Take care, son!" Mr. McFarlane said. The call ended and he looked down and closed his eyes. He had a slight smile but looked to be holding back tears.

"That was…" I started.

"My son…" Mr. McFarlane said, putting his phone back in his pocket and continuing to look out the window. The bluebird that landed there earlier proceeded to fly away. "I thought that I would never be able to see him again. Ten years in the CIA. Now he is on his way home."

The tears in his eyes were tears of joy. This was wonderful news for him. I didn't even know he had a son either! He had spent a decade with no family, losing his wife to cancer and then having to act like his son never existed, being undercover with the government and having no contact with the outside world. Now, he finally gets rewarded for his patience.

--- *One week later* ---

<BZZZT!>

My WCD was sitting on a charger in my room as I sat on the couch with one of my dad's old laptops. Hearing the incoming call, I set the laptop onto the coffee table and proceeded to make my way into my room to retrieve it. It was Mr. McFarlane.

"Shane speaking."

"Yes, Shane. I'd like you to meet me outside of town hall at about 3."

"What for?" I asked.

"I actually have two reasons." He said. "My son is going to meet me here. And they are also renaming the Municipal Center. That is when they are unveiling the new name. I encourage *all* AURORA members to attend. A general text will go out shortly."

"Got it!" I said. The call ended and I texted Hailey. "TOWN HALL AT 3."

It was about noon. My mom got off of work at 2, so it was possible that not only she could drive us but she would make it to this as well. I proceeded to sit back on the couch for the time being.

<KNOCK!><KNOCK!>

There was a knock on the door as I was waiting on a reply from Hailey. I got up from the couch and opened the door. Hailey looked at me with a smile. "Sorry, Shane!" she said. "This was easier than texting!"

"Probably just as well." I said. I stepped to the side to give her room to come in. As she stepped in, she closed the door behind her. "Mr. McFarlane said that he wants us all to meet at the town hall at 3. They are renaming the Municipal Center and he said we would want to be there for the big reveal. Not just that, but we are going to get to meet his son, who has been undercover with the CIA for the past 10 years. That is why we never knew about him."

Hailey's jaw dropped. "Wow…" she said in surprise. "He had a family this whole time?"

"His wife died in 2036…" I continued. "From cancer. He became more active with the community following that, and that seems to be also around the time that his son went off the radar."

She nodded her head and turned to look to the side as if she were trying to read her own thoughts. "A peculiar turn of events, this is." she said.

---2:45 PM---

My mom picked Hailey and I up and we made our way downtown. Most of those in attendance parked at Commerce Square and walked. As Hailey, my mom and I approached, we saw the others gathered around a decorative fountain in front of the town hall. There was a dark green sheet covering the top half above the entryway. *That must be where they have the new name*, I thought. Everyone was present. Gary and Veronica. Pablo and Maria. Mr. McFarlane and a man of about 178 centimeters who appeared to be in his 40s with brown hair, slightly hinting to gray. From the distance it looked like he was talking to Gary and Veronica, who were both in officer uniforms. There was some laughter so it was my guess he was probably an easygoing guy.

"Hey, nice to see you guys!" Veronica shouted as we approached. Everyone was exchanging hugs with us.

Mr. McFarlane looked over at us and then at his son. "Robert, I'd like you to meet, Shane, Hailey, and Shane's mom Patricia"

"Nice to meet you all!" Robert said with a cheerful smile, shaking hands with all of us in that order.

"You as well!" I said. "Mr. McFarlane kept your existence *well* hidden!"

Robert laughed. "Well, I would certainly hope so!" he said. "It was a matter of national security. He told me about that whole thing with the corruption here and Reginald Bergeron. I was stationed in Baltimore! So you guys helped me with *my* job and didn't even know it. I was undercover with his network with the express intent of exposing and breaking it up."

"And now it has been broken up." Hailey said.

Robert put his hand to his chin. "Hmm… exposed, yes. Broken up, no. But I guess the cage has been rattled enough to where the normal authorities could take it from here. So I get to go back to resuming a normal life and also have a pension from my work. Not quite an early retirement but close enough."

Mr. McFarlane looked over at him. "Just wait until you are my age and have three or four careers under your belt!" he said. He started cracking up.

I noticed that my mom hadn't said anything yet, but she seemed unusually content. "Are you ok, mom?" I asked.

She had a delayed reaction to my question, but looked at me and nodded her head with a smile. "I'm fine, Shane." She proceeded to look forward again, possibly observing her environment, but something told me it was more than that. I think Hailey sensed this because she pulled me to the side and whispered quietly into my ear.

"She has her eyes fixed on Robert…" Hailey said discreetly.

*Oh boy*, I thought. This was news that was completely out of left field for me. *I think it is way too soon to imagine myself having a stepfather*, I thought. But then again, it had been seven years since my dad passed. Seven years since my mom had even been with a man. She remained single this entire time. To her credit, that was a huge accomplishment. Maybe if she felt that she was ready, she deserved to be happy. *But for the love of God, don't rush!*

The day was mostly sunny, and it was almost directly overhead at about this time. I looked to my left where an adjacent street intersected with this one and saw a few bicycles, a few pedestrians, and even an old red car pass through. But there were at least 200 people in this area waiting for the great reveal. Maybe more. As this was on my mind, Officer Bigelow came out with a few other officers and government officials at his side. He carried a megaphone in his right hand.

"Ladies, gentlemen and people of Winchester! Thank you for your attendance! Today we are revealing the new name for our Municipal Center. As we continue to rebuild our lovely town from last year's tragic events, we thought that it would be fitting to honor one of our home grown who ended up giving his life in the effort to provide a path forward for all of us. So, it is my honor… to present to you, ladies, gentlemen and others, the Marco S. Rodriguez Municipal Center!"

At this point the green sheet fell from the building, revealing the full name. Those of us who knew all turned our gaze toward Pablo, who was in a state of shock. Maria appeared to pull him closer as he slowly cupped his hands over his face. He looked down as if he did not know whether to cry happy tears or sad tears.

"Take a deep breath!" Maria instructed. "It's ok!"

Pablo took a deep breath and straightened his posture, standing up straight and looking at the sign with tears in his eyes. He proceeded to do the sign of the cross with his right hand and then, with his eyes closed, put his hands over his heart.

The crowd noticing this emotion from him intensified their cheer after having learned of Pablo's attendance. After all, both of them were local celebrities in the college baseball world, and were on the verge of being drafted into the MLB at some point.

This event became a gathering for members of the community to get to know one another. While I was sure that many of the bad eggs had been eliminated over the past six months, I was still finding myself being a bit anti-social. Hailey was not much different in that. We remained with our normal group. Out of everyone, it seemed that Mr. McFarlane, Robert, Gary and Veronica were the most sociable. Pablo may have been if this event weren't too emotional for him. My mom found herself to be unusually timid as well. She and Robert were virtually the same age. Honestly he was probably the same age as my dad would have been had he been alive today. But seeing everything around me, I could tell that his presence was near us. The town was feeling united. The calm atmosphere that Officer Bigelow was promoting, which in turn eased the underlying fears held previously by most of us. The biggest factor was hope. Faith, hope and charity. It was as if the past members of AURORA were among us in the crowd. For a split second I thought I saw my dad, several meters away directing a smile in our direction. But I blinked on a double take and he was gone. I smiled and took a deep breath. For once, I was feeling happy about the life I was now living.

# CHAPTER 17

# All's Well That Ends Well

After the revealing at the town hall, things began to pick up in the community. 2046 has been a promising year so far and it is only April. There was a lot of talk on the topic of "What are we going to do now?" and such, especially among those of us at AURORA. It seemed like Hailey and I were the only ones without any real plans. Gary and Veronica are in the police force together under Officer Bigelow. Pablo and Maria are both on their baseball journeys. Once Pablo's suspended license became legal again, the Minnesota Twins were going to draft him. I didn't see why they would just take him anyway. He drives around not even caring that his license is suspended. While the new police force under Troy has made it safe, it also meant that traffic violations would be enforced again. I'd rather have a police force that sticks to the law than have a lawless police force. Mr. McFarlane has done well so far with his position in town hall, and Robert has been hired as an auditor to ensure that protocols are properly followed.

Hailey's parents offered me a job to work with them, and even my mother. Sometime in 2045 my mom's boss at the Shop N Rob got fired and someone more easy going entered the fold, but it was still a job that she did not care too much for. Most chain companies went through the government to pluck talent and fill vacancies, which is where the notion of "the government picks your job for you" comes along. My mom was forced into that system upon my father's death and had been there since. But in cases like Hailey's family, private companies, those who can afford to stay in business, still have the control that they did back in the old days. My mom had the idea of possibly expanding their business to include helping the local farm hands with their land, as that too can be considered "landscaping". There was no objection to this. Tim and Amber both were receptive to flexible, new ideas, so long as we were not spreading our resources too thin.

Mitch's warehouse was shut down and seized thanks to Maria submitting an "anonymous tip" to investigate that property. Gerald Cantrell was held responsible since nothing was legally in Mitch's name. Gerald ratted out Mitch for the dopamine emitter, and Mitch blamed Trent and Rico's deaths on Shannon. It was treachery on all sides for the remaining former League of Enlightment members, as the chaos of the missing information led to them all pointing fingers at one another in accusation. Because Mitch tampered with the original evidence, the entire scenario played out just as Pablo had predicted.

Chip and Lynn were arrested in association with the recent events and have been locked up locally, with Lynn also being charged with assault on Helen. Both Mitch and Shannon were transported out west to high security prisons where the lifers were serving. I could almost guarantee that they were not going to have it easy. We had heard from Helen at one point that her and Shannon's father Alex eventually killed their mother in self-defense and he is on suicide watch for the guilt of wasting his life with her and being an absent father. Our advice to her was to try to be understanding of him and at least try to win him over for the remainder of his life. So far, she and Viktor have been successful, but were also understandably reluctant to trust him. To think that I could have lived a similar life if Shannon and I ended up together. The thought made me shudder. No thanks.

*April 13, 2046*

Hailey and I were at my house playing checkers at the coffee table in the living room. It was around 9:30pm and my mom was working until 3am. We (obviously) hung out a lot but something felt different about tonight. There was a vibe in the room that I could not place my finger on. As Hailey took the lead on our game, the topic of conversation gravitated to that device that was at Mitch's Warehouse. With how traumatized she was with Officer Bergeron's violation of her, I was surprised that she had no such effect with the dopamine emitter. I was feeling hyper-vigilant in regards to her emotions since that day, not wanting to make the same mistake a second time that I did on the day of the debates. She would continually reassure me that she was fine and continue to be her confident self. At every turn, I was making my efforts to be attentive to her needs. Although I am sure that I am still in the middle of fine tuning this.

"What was even the point for that torture device?" I asked. I had a king near the far right corner of the board that was trying to run from one of Hailey's kings. I had two kings and three regulars still on the board and she had three kings and one regular.

"They were just being sadistic." Hailey said. She moved that same king on the board and looked up at me with a smirk. "How long are we going to play cat and mouse?" She asked.

I laughed, moving my king again. "You will have to corner me." I said.

Hailey began to back her pieces off in some kind of formation. "What was interesting about that device is… they hoped to ruin me sexually to get back at *you*... but it had the twofold side effect of making it easier for me to put the Bergeron incident behind me and making me more aware of my own impulses."

I raised my eyebrow. I moved my king one space down to the left, but one of her formation pieces was nearly in position to intercept it. "I… didn't think that was something that you could easily forget."

"It's not…" Hailey said. She proceeded to capture my runaway king on the board and looked up at me with a smile. "But I made myself a promise that, so long as I was conscious, that I would never allow myself to be subject to that again. I wanted so bad to *not* give them what they wanted that it became my strength to resist the device's capability to outright overtake me. Winning that battle restored my confidence. I know who I am… *and what I want.*"

She gazed at me with her *Pisces Eyes,* but it was accompanied by a smile. I nodded my head and grinned, looking down at the board. Her last statement was a reminder of the whole "thoughts dictate reality" phenomenon that she explained to me months ago. The warehouse was yet another example. I proceeded to move the regular piece forward that was on my side of the board. "You have no idea how proud that makes me…" I said. "Not just for me but… I admire your strength. You never were one to let anyone trample over you. I admire your assertiveness. Your confidence. I hold high esteem for you. After all we have been through… all *you* have been through… I find myself amazed by you. I… (looks up at her) am truly in love with you."

Hailey blushed and smiled at me as she proceeded to take my remaining king. All I had left were three regulars. She had all but won the game of checkers. "Why don't you… come with me for a moment."

*Ok*, I thought. I wasn't entirely sure why but I decided to go along with it. She seemed like she was about to head to the dining room where her bag was. I proceeded to follow her, but she stopped right at the edge of the room as I walked past her. I turned around to face her just in time for her to softly take my wrists and gently pin me against the wall behind me. My heart skipped a beat. *What's she doing?* I thought. She then pressed her body against mine, sandwiching me between her and the wall.

"Whoa…" I muttered. My heart began to race. *Is she making a move on me?* If this is the case, I am welcoming it.

Hailey proceeded to release my right wrist, but then pinned her wrist against it to hold me in place. She slid her hand behind my head and tilted me into position to kiss her. A makeout session started right then and there, with her continuing to gently compress me against the wall. Things were heating up fairly quickly. I felt myself getting insanely aroused. *Wow, Shannon has nothing on her*! Consent makes *all* the difference.

Hailey and I paused for a moment to breathe. She looked me in the eyes. "Would you like to play for a while?"

"Oh my god, yes!" I said. The enthusiasm behind my response was intense. My chest began to burn. I wanted to melt into a pool right at her feet. *I guess that makes me submissive*, I thought. As if this weren't obvious after the New York incident. Shannon was particularly dominant as well, but while she seemed great at the time, the thought of the experience aged like milk. Hailey had me where she wanted me, and I *wanted it* that way.

"Good." Hailey said with a smile, gently touching my cheek and then reinforcing her pin on me. "I hope to show you how to read hints, though. I gave you two earlier and you were oblivious."

I would analyze this later. My focus was on her. We proceeded to make out some more as she began grinding on me. Our hands found one another as they were raised high against the wall, our fingers intertwining. I felt my body quivering from the excitement stirring within me. I was absolutely certain that she felt the same way. She then took a step back, still holding my hands. There was a fire in her eyes as she stared into mine. “Bedroom. Now.” She said with a playful smile.

She released my left hand and proceeded to pull me in the direction of my room, leading the way. We quickly made our way in and closed the door.

*[Soundtrack song for ending credits: New Politics - We are the Radio]*

# ***Epilogue***

*July 9, 2062*

If I could write this to my younger self, I would. So much has happened. Just when you think things are hopeless, life has its way of surprising you. After my 17th birthday I had genuinely become afraid that I was going to lose Hailey. I am forever thankful that she held on and was patient with me, and we both grew closer and stronger from the experience. It was bad enough that she and I were awkward on the topic of sex because of Shannon's impact on our relationship. Did that make things more difficult? At times it did, but because that wasn't the entire basis of our relationship, we survived the assault coming at us from both Bergeron and Shannon. We had mutually agreed to hold off as long as we could, since we did not know what kind of world that we would potentially bring our kids into, and we also didn't know if our adversaries would be around to sabotage it. When everything came to a conclusion in April 2046, we finally consummated our relationship. It was exactly as she and I had hoped. Like how our relationship transitioned from friendship to romance two years earlier, we wanted this to just sort of happen spontaneously on its own. That night, she wanted me. I wanted her. The mutual consent made the experience absolutely fulfilling. Hailey has always been a better initiator, but I would learn from her over time. We had our moments. Things would be hot and things would be cold. But we never took it personally and we supported one another through it. And there have been so many other ways to connect that we haven't been given the opportunity to doubt our love and commitment to one another. We don't put all of our eggs in one basket.

It wasn't long before Hailey was pregnant with our first child. On April 26, 2047, our son Caleb was born, and on June 2, 2051, she gave birth to our daughter Kylie. Caleb is smart and curious, much like a mix of both Hailey and I, but he is absolutely stubborn at times. He takes after me with regards to questioning everything and seems to take on the role of a young philosopher. Kylie is that quiet girl and an absolute bookworm. She found that she has a talent for music and can already play both a piano and a keyboard. While her classmates listen to pop music, she is over here listening to classical music like Mozart or Chopin. She has been called a nerd in school for her thick rimmed glasses, but we are all incredibly supportive of her and she has begun to own her identity. Both of our kids can hold intelligent conversations with adults, and this is something we take pride in. Caleb and Kylie both share in our neurodivergencies as well, and our understanding of ourselves and each other has helped us to build an environment for them in which they can thrive and feel safe.

My mom, 62, still lives in the same house. In fact, Hailey and I decided to move in to my mom's house and when Kylie was born, we all pitched in and had an addition built on. Hailey and I have our own room upstairs now, across from my mom's room. Caleb ended up with my old room that was connected to the living room. We knocked out the south wall of the dining room and built Kylie's room there. Hailey and I work with her parents still on their landscaping, and will one day inherit their business. But for now, things are as harmonic as they were in the 40s. My mom ended up doing volunteer work and, as fate would have it, she ended up running into Robert on a constant basis. Hailey and I low key predicted this, of course. After a few years of being friends, in 2049 they actually decided to date. Even Mr. McFarlane began teasing them when they started hanging out together. They never married and he never moved in, but he does come over frequently and they have their own system going. What matters is that they are happy. I guess when you are older and have been through the ringer, you are far more passive on whether or not you marry or live with them. My mom's health has improved to levels not seen since my dad was still alive, and she has been happy for quite some time now. I just saw her chasing the kids around the yard yesterday and she wasn't even out of breath. I'm so proud of her.

On a sadder note, in 2057, Mr. McFarlane died peacefully in his sleep at the age of 85. He had his good health all the way up until he was about 81. The last four years of his life were spent with him getting restricted to a walker and his voice getting weaker. That was about the time he retired from public service as well. Nobody was sure about what caused his health to take a nosedive like it did, although the winter of 2053 was extremely brutal for our region. By the time it warmed back up outside, he was never the same. On Hailey's 31st birthday, Mr. McFarlane made it known that his dying wish was to visit HQ one more time, even to the point of seeing his name appear on the hand print screen. Hailey and I helped him down the stairs with his walker and we helped him guide his shaky hand to the hand print. The good old *MCFARLANE, JOHN C. --APPROVED.* Appeared. When he came in, all of us were waiting for him. My mom watched everyone's kids for the day while Gary, Veronica, Pablo and Maria met us there. Knowing it would be his last time there, he took one last look around, and then after Hailey and I helped him sit on one of the couches, the rest of us surrounded him on the other couches. He had made an impromptu speech, which Hailey managed to transcript (She really has a talent for doing that!).

*"Today is March 4, 2057... as you guys probably know, my time is running out. But, I want you to know that I have been truly blessed to know each and every one of you in my lifetime. Those present, those past, and those who were unable to make it today. It has been an honor and a privilege to serve our community. It is a bittersweet feeling... knowing that this will be the last time that I set foot in HQ... having spearheaded the AURORA organization some 45 years ago. But I could not think of a better group of people to whom I will leave my legacy... my life's work...* our *life's work. My dying wish was to be able to meet like this... one last time with you all."*

Mr. McFarlane would break down into tears after saying this, and all of us comforted him and reassured him. There wasn't a dry eye in the room. All of us were prepared, including Mr. McFarlane himself. But we wanted nothing more than to send him off to the cosmos having had his wishes fulfilled. He would pass away a month later, barely making it past his 85th birthday on March 25. We archived his final entries into the system in his memory while we were there together for the last time.

*1301 MCFARLANE, JOHN C. -IN- 2057/03/04*<br>
*1422 MCFARLANE, JOHN C. -OUT- 2057/03/04*

Pablo, 39, is still playing pro baseball and alternates between center and right field for the Minnesota Twins. He somehow managed to remain with the same team his entire career and is a 10 time All-Star. His college nickname of "D-Man" seemed to stick when he transitioned to the major leagues. All of us are still particularly close to Pablo, and he and Maria agreed to be the Godparents of our kids if anything were to happen to Hailey and I.

Maria, 35, retired from baseball after getting shot in her throwing arm while at a bar a few years ago. She played shortstop for the Florida Marlins. It just so happened that during the 2058 season, she was in the wrong place at the wrong time, and two bar patrons got into a fight and one of them pulled out a gun. The man who would've been the victim ended up grabbing the arm of the man who had the gun and inadvertently caused him to pull the trigger, the bullet lodging in the rotator of Maria's right arm. Since then she hasn't been able to use that arm for anything other than light activity. It was a particularly demoralizing event since she was one of the first females to ever play in the MLB, and, like Pablo had years earlier, she was just starting to reach her peak as a professional ball player. Because of her petite size and actually being a *short*stop, she was known around the league as "The Mouse." or even "Mini Mouse". She and Pablo are still romantically involved, but are waiting until both of them are retired before starting a family together.

Gary, 36, and Veronica, 35, are both still cops. We don't hear from them as much as we used to, but we are still in touch. They got a house over in Pablo's neighborhood on the east side. They have two kids, daughter Daria (10) and son David (8). Both of them started getting involved with the church as well and do a lot of missionary work. They still work under Troy Bigelow, who remains our police chief. We have seen our fair share of peace and harmony these last 15 years or so, but now and again we keep coming across people trying to creep from the woodworks looking to watch the world burn all over again. Troy was quoting "It is our job to provide nothing for the fire to consume so that it has nowhere to go but out." In 2051, a group of religious fanatics stopped into town and tried to destroy Troy's credibility by slandering him for his sexual orientation. Troy would later go on record as saying "I have never hid that part of me from the public. Who I choose for a partner in my personal life has absolutely no impact on my ability to perform my duties as police chief." Given that we are a town out in the middle of nowhere, I was actually surprised at the amount of support that he received in response to this. His professionalism was untouchable by almost every other public figure you could think of. I remember Hailey seeing this on TV, looking at me with her hands out going "Who the hell cares? It's his life!" I agreed. Being a public figure shouldn't bar anyone from the right to be themselves.

Lastly, in 2058, we had a bit of a surprise. Helen's family moved back into town, ironically back into her childhood home. Her Uncle Viktor had passed away in 2051 and her dad in 2056. Every once in a while we meet at the park for a picnic, letting the kids run around and the adults sit at a table talking about life's latest. Her husband Kaiden is a pretty upstanding guy. He actually works for the Fire Department. When Hailey and I told him about the addition we made to our house, he offered to inspect it to make sure that it was up to code, which it was. Helen is a nurse at the Northside Hospital, something she was inspired to get into after the turf war of 2046. Their daughter Melissa is now a student at Winchester High and shares a couple of classes with Caleb. The two of them are friends, but we have been keeping a close eye on both of them in case sparks fly. Melissa's birthday is Nov. 18, 2044, two years ahead of Caleb. Caleb is probably too close minded and stubborn and would need to work on his maturity anyway. Melissa has emotional mood swings and seems to have a darkness about her that I related to when I was her age, except she seems to fit more into a gothic/alternative clique; dressing in black and the tattoos and piercings and such. Not that we were going to judge, but knowing Caleb, he could make things toxic. We can't control whether or not they hang out at school, but outside of that we make the rules.

Saving the crapshoot for last, last I knew, both Chip and Lynn, 36, remained in prison for their association to the activities they engaged in back in the mid-2040s. Gerald Cantrell did not end up going to prison but he lost his business to shareholders and was the center of scandal until his death in 2054. Mitch and Shannon are still alive, miraculously, still in their respective maximum security prisons. Shannon actually had the nerve to try to write us an unprovoked letter in 2051. We did not respond but it was more or less her trying to apologize for her "misdeeds" and seeing if she could find a way to rope us back into her life. *Nope.* Not falling for that shit. When I told Helen about this later, without hesitation she said that I made the right choice. Reginald Bergeron was found hanging in his prison cell in 2051, having committed suicide. In regards to where our remaining adversaries are located, I do know that they are all separated and none of them are in the same correctional facility. That's actually a good thing. As we had learned from Mitch and Chip, all it takes is for a mere two of them to congregate for everything to start all over again. God help us if any of them start planning anything while behind bars.

www.ingramcontent.com/pod-product-compliance
Lightning Source LLC
LaVergne TN
LVHW010657110826
845149LV00014B/3129

* 9 7 9 8 9 8 8 8 9 8 6 2 7 *